TEMPLE OF LUST

TEMPLE OF LUST

JOHN BURTON THOMPSON

CUTTING EDGE

ISBN-13: 978-1-954840-62-1

Published by
Cutting Edge Books
PO Box 8212
Calabasas, CA 91372
www.cuttingedgebooks.com

FOREWORD

This is a work of fiction in a factual setting, a setting as absorbing and romantic as any known to man. It is amazing how many *Norteamericanos* familiar with the culture of ancient Egypt seem virtually unaware of an equally ancient culture much closer to home, in many ways more advanced and, to me, more interesting—that of the Mayan peoples of Yucatan, Guatemala and points south.

Where did they come from? How did they develop a calendar superior to our own? What genius among them first developed the concept of zero—key to their mathematical system, and the basis of any higher mathematics? These are but a few of the tantalizing questions evoked by any contact with Mayan culture and history.

Doubtless my own eyes, like those of so many of my countrymen, would still remain closed to the Mayan magic were it not for my good fortune in making—while visiting Yucatan—some of the finest friends a man could have. Among other things, they took the trouble to disclose to me the wonders of the Maya. To them, certainly, warmest acknowledgement is due.

And so, I express here my sincere thanks to Don Fernando Barbachano, Sr., and his son, Fernando Barbachano, Jr., for their generous assistance—and, incidentally, for permission to use their names in this volume. For the same reasons, thanks go to José Mercader and my excellent friend, Pepe.

I give thanks also to Manuel Cirerol-Sansores, the author of *Chi-Cheen Itsa,* for the information and inspiration I received from his fine book.

Thanks are given, further, to Mario Molina, his beautiful cousin, Anita De Palma, and her parents, Señor and Señora Mendez, all of who encouraged and helped in that open-handed manner peculiar to our Latin neighbors.

Especial appreciation goes to the wonderful Camara-Peon family, too, for their aid and their unforgettable hospitality. And my thanks, finally, are extended to all my other friends in Yucatan, unnamed here, but whose courtesies and warm hearts I shall never forget.

John B. Thompson

CHAPTER ONE

THE IRON HORSE is a modest enough sort of joint. The bourbon tastes something like whiskey should taste after being operated upon by Kentucky's magicians, so I had been going there during my too long sojourn in that city of bronze monuments and drafty mausoleums, Washington.

I had been there working for Uncle for six months on a deal wherein a foreign government was nibbling away at certain important bureau personnel by using that best of bait, lucre, and they seemed to be geniuses at picking guys and gals who didn't have any to speak of.

The Iron Horse is close enough to Union Station and the capitol and an office building I had been patronizing so that I could bibe and not lose too much time. In fact, a goodly number of other government employees, some of whom could afford more and better bourbon than I, patronized the bar and, of course, there was a sprinkling of those who couldn't afford but bought anyway. And there were still others who couldn't afford to have the stuff inside them.

"Bourbon and branch," I told Mike, the squatty red-faced Irishman with not quite enough hair on his head to make wings for a glass Christmas tree bird.

"Takes all kinds," bassed Mike in a voice that made his ranks of glasses dance. "Take me, I'd ruther rye and Coke."

"In that case," I said, having heard his preferences before, "I'd suggest that you drink rye and Coke."

"I does," said Mike with a surprised look on his geezer. "Always does. Of course I mean when I ackshully drink."

"That's what I thought you meant."

"Huh?"

"I said that's what I thought you meant."

"Oh, yeah. Sure. That's what I meant." Great conversationalist, Mike.

There was a silence during which I made inroads in my bourbon and branch and Mike mopped the bar automatically. Finally he came close and leaned across the bar and said in a low roar, "A frail's givin' you the lamp."

I didn't look around. I looked at Mike. "What frail?"

He shrugged. "How'm I to know? A frail's a frail to me."

"Not by a long shot," I assured him. "A frail is definitely not always a frail. She might be a robin, or a quail, or even a titmouse."

Mike took another casual glance. "This'n you might could call a titmouse, if you get what I mean. And I do mean it."

I got what he meant and in so doing became interested. I'm a man who is always highly interested in the titmice variety of women, especially when so described by Mike who is inclined to be literal at times.

I could catch a glimpse of her in the mirror and though the glimpse was of nothing more than a length of nylon-clad leg it was plenty. The leg was turned so delicately from such fabulous materials, one automatically expected it to be fragile, but it was too solidly fleshed for that. Good, well-nurtured, vitaminized flesh with healthy milk-fed bone as reinforcement and an ankle that was sheer witchery. No body, I reasoned, could possess such a leg without certain other projections being equally fine in quality.

She was almost directly behind me and seated in a booth. The Iron Horse boasts two booths with a jukebox that doesn't play between them; this titmouse, seated in the one behind me, put me at a disadvantage. If I turned around to look it would be obvious enough to anyone who happened to be watching; such brashness is not my way. Instead I thought of a brasher move that had some elements of frankness in it and which seemed in better taste. I paid for my drink and slid casually from the stool; then I walked directly to the booth. I had trouble with the last three steps because by then she had registered and if I'd been a cash register I'd have stripped every gear in my system. Being of a stouter mold I just sort of bent inward mentally and held on to my aplomb with both fists.

"Good morning," I said, flashing her a set of teeth of which I'm proud.

Her ripe red lips curved in a little smile and she showed me what a sorry set of teeth I had. "Good morning."

She gave forth with sounds that should have been recorded on Victor Red Seal.

"The bartender," I continued, "is a Mick with no soul and seems to think you were desirous of closer acquaintance with me and this is the only way to really find out."

"In this case your bartender is a man with a great soul and even greater perception. He was quite correct and I must say subtle. I didn't think he was noticing me and I didn't see him communicate with you." There was a queer adolescent bookishness to her speech, but I didn't care. Just so long as she kept talking.

"Do you think I'm horridly forward?" she asked, her liquid mellow tones making my skin itch.

"Oh, possibly forward, but not horridly so. You have the sort of touch, a kind of divinity that makes ordinarily horrid things delightfully correct. After all, if you wanted to meet me what would it profit either of us to play proper? This might never have happened."

"I'm glad it did," she said softly, "and, of course, you're right. I'm Dayne Holcombe."

"I'm Chester Markham. Ches to my friends, among whom you've suddenly elevated yourself to the upper skimming. Dayne—I've never heard that before. Lovely."

She looked at me for a moment to see if I were trying to kid her. It happened that I wasn't and she saw it. It impressed her and for a moment she breathed through slightly parted lips. While the momentary silence sat on us I used the time to weigh her out in a number of different ways. She tipped plenty on every scale. She was pink-bronze—that's the best way to describe her coloring. Her hair was a reddish bronze in dim light that would seem almost blonde in the daylight and it would gleam like metal. Her skin had been kissed by the sun until it married the color of her hair. Her wrists and hands were also a faint golden bronze and the long-sleeved high-necked dress was just a shade off bronze, toward white. It seemed to fit her superlative structure with a breathtaking touch of just-rightness and the curve that started at her waist and swept upward to the richly pointed protrusions of her breasts was a thing of the purest delight.

Her eyes fell as she realized that I'd been giving her the assessment; a little wave of pink swept upward from her neckline. Her skin also seemed so soft and fine that it should be fragile but the richness of her coloring mitigated that impression.

"Surely," I said gently, "you're not ashamed of being beautiful?"

Her eyes came up again and I could see that they were the color of violets, dewy and as clear and unclouded as a spring morning. "No, I'm not ashamed, really. It's just that scrutiny always makes me uncomfortable."

"Then you must exist in a constant state of discomfort."

Her laugh was silvery. "I can see that my instinct was not amiss. You're a really delightful person, Ches."

"I grow on people. Now, tell me something. If I'd seen you I think I should have tried meeting you for a whole slew of reasons. Just what did you have in mind when you gave me the eye?"

Her smile was as warm as a summer sun and a little involuntary shift made something hiss deep in a hidden recess, like the gentle rasping of silk against silk. "Are you trying to make small of your own attractions?"

"Well, I'd never thought of my possessions as being all that attractive and I might mention that a lot of women agree with me."

"And a lot of them disagree as greatly as I do. Admit it."

I grinned. "Oh, a couple, maybe."

Her eyes became fixed as she ticked off my good points. "You have nice hair …"

"Hold it. I have hair the color of wheat straw and nearly as coarse. It stands up like a boar's ruff and nothing I can do ever makes it lie down."

She ignored me. "Your skin is burned almost the color of an Indian, you have the nicest blue eyes that crinkle with laugh wrinkles at the corners. I like that little crooked grin of yours. It slants in the same direction as your nose.

"Crack-up," I said, "not fists. I keep fists out of my face."

"You were in the Air Corps?"

"Yeah. World War Two and Two-and-a-Half."

She folded her arms, making soft delicious dents in her breasts. "And you're big without being too big. I don't like men of football-player size."

"I've played."

"Yes, but you're the breakaway halfback, not the tackle and guard type."

"End," I corrected.

"Same thing. They have to be very fast and able to kick well."

I looked at my watch. "Look, I have an appointment with a guy about a game of tennis. If I could catch him I'd phone and cancel it but I can't, so—when will I see you again?"

Her eyes were steady. "You can see me whenever you wish, Ches. Tonight, maybe?"

"Well, I have something on tonight, but it can wait. Where?"

"Will you call for me at my apartment? Then we can decide what we'll do."

"Right."

"I live in Chevy Chase. It's just a block off Blackledge at 4801 Price. Apartment two-thirteen."

I made a swift etching. "Got it."

"Aren't you going to write it down?"

"Nope. I memorize things."

"My, what a smart man you are."

"Gift. And now, Dayne, I must tear myself away, although I never hated anything worse. I'll call you before I come."

"Please do. I'll be waiting." Her face went suddenly serious. "Waiting, Ches."

I squeezed her hand and went through the door beside the bar where I waited for five minutes, smoking a cigarette; then I peeked out. She was gone so I came out and went back to the bar.

"Geez, what a line," rumbled Mike, pouring a shot of bourbon and branch.

"And what a titmouse, Mike."

"You can say that again. Shoulda seen 'em move when she walked."

"Shame on you for such language. How long had she been there when you saw her eyeing me?"

"She was here when you come in. Why?"

"She's phony."

Mike goggled. "Her, phony? I'd say she's class all the way to the top of the Monument."

I nodded. "I don't mean anything against her class. She's got that, all right."

"I don't get you."

"She did. That is, that's how come she was here."

"What the hell for?"

"Ah. That comes in the next chapter, as they say in books."

"I never read no books."

"You should. No end enlightening on things and stuff."

"How'd you tumble to her?"

"She knows I played football. She had been briefed on it but not well enough. She went a little too far when she said an end had to be a good kicker. Any high school kid knows better than that."

"I seen an end kick once."

"Me too, but a coach doesn't rate his ends by their kicking ability. Hello, what's that."

Mike looked. "Scrap of paper."

I got up, walked over and picked it up. It was typewritten and had a good description of me written singlespaced. It was plain note paper that had been folded and creased tightly several times. She must have been studying it and missed her purse when she put it away. Maybe it had been my fault for turning and walking over to her so suddenly.

I skated it across the gleaming bar and Mike read it, moving his lips. "Geez! She knowed you."

"Nope, but she was looking for me."

"What you reckon that means?"

"I don't know—but I'll find out, I hope."

Mike shook his head. "Bad times around here now—just like them guys what jumped you up there by the Willard that night."

That had been a neat bit of luck. I had my dope and we were all ready to make arrests, but we knew the best we could get was deportation and the chief didn't like it. He had been a tough cop once and to him there was only one type of crook that you could deal with—the kind on a cold slab. He had put a few there himself because, as he said, he was scared of them. There's little doubt that if he hadn't been scared he'd have been a long time dead because he had not only a rugged reputation but he was smart; that's a bad combination for the opposition.

Now he's the boss of a Washington bureau that handles a lot of touch-me-not situations. I guess you could call us undercover

Q-guys since we're nominally under that branch, but whenever there's a loaded situation we get the call as long as it is small enough for us to handle. Anything of a really big nature is always handled through the top office.

These birds jumped me that night and we made the welkin ring. Luckily it was late and we were the only ones on the street, else someone would surely have been in the way. I grew up in Texas where you bite on Colts instead of teething rings and there's still a lot of deluded people who think that a gun in the hand means you're armed. Not necessarily. These fellows might have done fine with sawed-off shotguns, but they hit everything on the street with their shots—except me. I didn't hit anything except them.

Mike was right. Things were a little tense. I went over to the bureau office four blocks down Pennsylvania Avenue and walked in on Frank Barber who was throwing a letter opener at a drawing of a plush gal he had pinned to the back of a government chair. He was hitting her with piquant accuracy, too.

"Siddown," he rumbled, "and don't disturb me."

"It comes with old age," I said.

He straightened up after retrieving the knife and put it on his desk. "It comes with being bored. I'd like to go out and smoke up some joint." He patted a little oil from his shiny bald head. He was short and thick but he hadn't gone much to flesh even at his age. His face was square, honest and tough. His eyes were a mild deceptive grey. He licked his lips. "What's on your mind?" I showed him the little square of paper. He took it and read it. "What's this, ego masturbation?"

"A frail dropped it. Mike calls her a frail, but she ain't all that frail. She's classic and very unfrail in selected areas."

"Who selects 'em?"

"Me. I've never been known to be wrong."

"Might be false."

"That's for adolescents. I got genius in that line. I can spot 'em a mile off."

"She make up to you?"

"In a way. Very genteel and all."

"Offer to give you any?"

"Don't be crude."

"Who?"

"You."

"Oh. Well, that wasn't crude. I asked you a question."

"There was the vaguest suggestion that I might be able to tickle her on the ankle."

"That's being uncrude, I guess. Think there's any connection between her and Kaav?"

"Can't say. What do they want now?"

"Can't say, unless they want to stretch you out like you did their buddies. By the way, the Cheese wants you for a conference in the morning at ten."

"What's on his mind?"

"He didn't say, but he sounded serious."

"Goody. Now I won't get bored, maybe."

"Wish he'd call me. Wish anyone'd call me if it was nothing but to get a cat out of a tree."

"Shall I put one up a tree and call you?"

"You're being cute and insubordinate now. I could fire you."

"Maybe the Cheese will do it for you."

"Did you make a date with this frail?"

"Well, let's say we collaborated on a date. As I recall she wanted to seem anxious without seeming anxious."

"Did she make it?"

"Perfect. I might have been proud of the job myself. By that time I was ready to bite at the first opportunity."

"And you bit?"

"I bit. She lives at the Stoddard Apartments in Chevy Chase, 4801 Price. I tell you that in case I turn up missing for the appointment in the morning."

"I'll turn the joint inside out," he said. "I'll search every house in the neighborhood and frighten every grandma and kid in Chevy Chase. Frank Barber to the rescue."

"Don't try to be prophetic."

"I'm not. I'm just romancing. She'll turn out to be some one hundred percent American girl with a one hundred percent case of over-heated breeches who'll love the one hundred percent b'jesus out of you and send you back to me all hollow-eyed and anemic looking."

"Tired but happy," I supplied.

"I hate your damned argot," he said passionlessly.

"Gives mustard to casual speech."

"I'd like to put mustard in your underdrawers."

"Well, if you have nothing for me but insults I think I'll go along. By the way, she isn't a one hundred percent American girl at all, she's furren."

"How do you know?"

"She thinks an end on a football team has to be able to kick. G'bye."

"Hey, wait. You on the level about that?"

"Sure."

His shaggy grey brows came together. "That makes a difference. Call me on the hour, will you? All the time you're there."

"You sound concerned."

"I'd rather be now than later when you can't be found except for an ear or a finger."

"Thanks."

"Don't mention it."

CHAPTER TWO

I HAD a place on Eighth Street that was presided over by a small swarthy gent name of Alonso Pizarro. I inherited Lonzo from the Border Patrol although said Patrol never knew it because when I first saw Lonzo he was a "wetback" literally fresh out of the Rio Grande and the BPs were hard on his cold trembling tail. He was wizened, pathetic and his only crime that of trying to find the means of filling his capacious little belly, so I put him under a robe in the back of my convertible and went home with him. Later we legalized him, or he legalized himself by joining the Navy. After several years of strife he came out looking as sleek and fat as a prize Angus steer. There was a certain "to hell with you" swagger to his walk and a proud lift to his head that made you sort of happy for the little fellow because you could see that he was happy for himself. He had turned into a poker bug during the war and might have bought a sizable hunk of Chihuahua with his takings but, as he put it, he had fallen in love with his benefactor and was never so happy as when hanging around seeing said benefactor did as little by way of manual labor as was humanly possible. At that particular job he was a genius. Like a Chinaman he had everything in the joint so filed as to be the only one who could find what I required.

He was a superlative cook and early in our association had also discovered that I was a man to whom there was only one never-failing attraction, the female of the species. So, in addition to my stomach and other creature comforts, he assumed the role of gentleman procurer and I must say that he had an eye for class even though his operating strata was necessarily restricted. He really did nobly by me within the confines of his sphere.

Even in Washington he had managed to locate some very tender and delectable subjects and, knowing my aversion to the professionals, he had shocked me several times by the youth and obvious amateurishness of his finds who made up in vigor and eagerness what they lacked in polish. I wended my way home that afternoon in a dark brown study having to do with the elegant and not too clever Dayne. I had met her kind of Mata Hari before, but Dayne was tender and succulent like a hot house grape, intelligent but definitely not clever—unless her cleverness took the form of naiveté. That could be because she had been as wide open as a church clock from the very start. If her interest was pretense then I didn't know women; it would have hurt to admit that, although I realize I don't know all by a long shot. Moreover, she was the type who fell flat when she tried any sort of cute shrewdness, just as she had when she got over her head in the tangles of football.

That little mistake only branded her as something not of our shores or someone who had been too sheltered. Her English was perfect, a little too perfect and sterile of slangisms. She didn't talk like a nineteen-year-old who had had free access to the Four Freedoms and a few others not so heavily conceived. My mouth watered a little as I reconstructed her in my mind's eye and tasted anew the superb sculpture of her body as it slipped a little beneath the rich material of her dress. She moved, Mike had said, and of course she would, walking woman-like with hard-heeled assertiveness. She was certainly latent motherhood in every respect, nor was her perfect back marred by a bra strap cutting into the flesh, which is a dead giveaway as to what will happen when support is removed. If she wore support at all it was merely a concession to the times, not a necessity.

My apartment is a member of that Washington red brick clan jammed shoulder to shoulder like old men leaning together to keep from falling. I have wondered idly what would happen if one of them burned out. Would the others collapse?

I thought of my ranch house that sprawled over an acre and a half of Texas—roomy, quiet and not even a step from the ground to the porch. You just walk in, not up. I had a two-flight walk-up stint facing me and I didn't like it. Lonzo had never discovered a means by which to remove that bit of annoyance.

I was puffing when I walked into the cream plastered living room with old prints on the walls—good ones, I had been told, and if age is any criterion they were masterpieces. I hadn't been attracted enough to notice what they represented, being more disposed to a tremendous Mexican calendar Lonzo had erected in the kitchen that was a riot of color with some Aztec bravo hovering over an Aztec maid half-hidden in lush grass, looking a little disheveled and breathless and potent in the indicated places. It had a Spanish caption that read simply, "Boy and Girl and Love."

At any rate, thanks to that keen appreciation which is indigenous to Mexicans there was certainly no missing ingredient. There was a mountain far in the background, Popocatapetl no doubt, but Popocatapetl has a long spotless history of letting love and boys and girls severely alone and it was not intruding on these.

I flopped on a nice light blue couch and seemed to hear the faint silky hiss of Dayne's clothes as she shifted her body in the booth and I was all ready to go over the whole thing again when Lonzo put his swarthy head in and grinned at me. "And a rare good afternoon to you."

"It is neither rare nor good as far as I can see," I said. "What's for dinner?"

"Lamb chops broiled with bacon, sherry mint sauce and plenty of cayenne. Whipped potatoes, broccoli, hot rolls and iced tea and a salad."

"Ummm." I swallowed and nodded. "Sounds passable. Would you object if I fixed myself a drink?"

"No, because I'm up to my *cabeza* in the rolls at the moment."

When I picked him up that chill night half dead from cold and wet he knew about six English words which he worked to death. Now he had an accent, but it was too slight to reproduce. He was talkative as all get out and inclined at times to disregard his position as a servant. He ate with me and would probably have slept with me except I snore to beat hell and kick, too.

He came back after I had built me a highball, wiping his arms and hands on a cloth. "Didn't you wind up this cloak and dagger deal the other day?"

"Right."

"Then what're we hanging around here for winter to catch us for?"

"Something else seems ready to come up. Furthermore, as you can recall from your Navy days, you go where you're told, not where pleasure beckons, when you work for Uncle."

He nodded, but paid no attention to what I had said. "Cousin Ramon writes that a family has moved in from Corpus with six daughters, each more beautiful than the other no matter which end you start at."

"You mean they look like a modern automobile?"

Lonzo blushed a little. "I was referring to the six daughters, not an approach to any one of them in the singular."

"Oh! I see now."

"I suspect that you saw at first but you're a little willful about such things at times."

"You should have seen the titmouse I located today."

"Washington is loaded," he said carelessly, "but they're not our kind. This climate makes their buttocks pimply and many of them have sinus trouble. Poorest pickings I've seen."

I cringed a little. "You're blunt, all right, but there isn't a pimple on this babe."

"Ah, you explored?"

"No." I think maybe I blushed a little because his grin was satanic. "There just can't be."

"Pimples," he said dogmatically. "Betcha. You'll see her again?"

"Tonight."

"So? Wanna bet?"

"No," I yelled, "and fix me another drink since your *cabeza* is out of the rolls."

I didn't call her as I promised but got in my car, drove on out to Chevy Chase, and parked a block from her place. I was early and under my arm was two and a half pounds of confidence that had been fashioned by the Colt people, in a special holster. I had on a pair of blue flannels with a darker blue coat loose-fitting on purpose.

The building just escaped being pretentious because it was of buff brick, not too big and probably full of these efficiency cubicles that make you think you're living in an outsize clothes hamper.

I located her button but the old caution still prevailed and I punched another one under the name of Miss Agatha Creech and the speed with which the lock reacted was indicative of something. Luckily Miss Agatha's apartment was on another floor and I wouldn't have to duck her when no one appeared and she started searching.

When I got opposite Dayne's door I was struck with several peculiar things. First, the door wasn't quite closed, leaving a crack not even wide enough to see inside but wide enough to permit the sounds of several blows and a soft whimpering cry.

Zounds and so forth in the Galahad tradition. A maid was being murdered. I whammed the door open and got a glimpse of slim lovely legs all the way to where they weren't legs any more, the fusion being obscured by a breathless gesture of white fitting like a paint job. She had rolled with another slap and her skirt flared up momentarily. A very foreign-looking egg, who had already slapped her enough so that her face was red, whirled as I came in and went into his clothes for an equalizer of some sort which I didn't care to face. On the other hand, I couldn't see outing my own cannon and blasting up enough furor to take another day to quell so I kicked him. I really threw that foot and the shock of it traveled all the way up to my watch pocket. He went backward, struck the well-sprung couch and rebounded. As he came forward I splintered his dentures with another kick and left him writhing on the dark blue carpet, bubbling unhappily through blood and stumps of shattered teeth.

I bent over her. "Did he hurt you?"

Her eyes were stark with fear but she shook her head slowly. Her lips kept saying, "Go, go, go …" I hadn't heard that since the days of "Go, go, go for a touchdown."

"What's this all about?"

"Oh … Ches …" She put her hands to her face and sobbed brokenheartedly while I wished for some other castle to pull down for her.

One was coming up behind me but I never knew that, of course, because the lights went out in a brief burst of raw jagged pain.

I came back enough for voices to make some impression. Also I had the impression that I was in a chair, the damnedest uncomfortable arrangement of sticks and rungs I had ever sat in. I didn't want to fight or struggle or do anything but sleep— which wasn't in the program. They kept slapping me awake and a voice like nails on a blackboard kept asking me questions. I didn't know any answers and told them so over and over. There was a loss of patience and the slap wasn't a slap any more but a very painful fist. Not as painful as it might have been if I hadn't been so sleepy.

A girl had hysterics and screamed at the top of her voice. There was the sound of another blow and silence on her part.

Then a professional voice. "This stuff doesn't fail. He doesn't know anything."

"If the information I've been given is incorrect," said Raspy, "someone will be sorry."

"Better check it again," said Professional. "I've used this technique before and it's good. He's been telling you the whole truth."

A mumbling broke out that was as jagged as broken glass with fury. I couldn't make out what he was saying but he was mad and having trouble with his speech.

"Silence," said Raspy. "No one gave you permission to beat her. She had followed orders. I don't care a rap about your amours and jealousy. Nor do I intend to tell you all my plans. She had this man to her apartment at my orders. From your appearance I should judge that Mr. Markham is a fairly good man with his fists—or feet, as you insist. No more than you deserve."

There was more spitty grumbling and the sound of a sharp crack and the mumbling ceased simultaneously with the sound of a thud on the floor.

I managed to get my eyes open. Raspy was thin but of the whalebone type of thinness, tall and very dark. His eyes were slitted and opaque as lumps of coal. His lips were cruel and bloodless. Professional was a black-and-white-clad doctor who had been on bad times. He was wattled and wasted. A shell of a man. Dayne was slumped on a cheap lumpy couch sobbing quietly, her bronze hair spread out in a mess that was still lovely. She wore something in white that was wrinkled and smudged now, but no amount of dishabille could obscure the subtle fit. My other pal was dragging himself off the floor.

The room was rather bare with cankered walls and paper as ancient as grapes and cupids. On the floor was a tattered carpet and somewhere water dripped dismally. My arms and back ached and now I knew why. They were tied, as were my legs, hard to the chair.

Raspy turned to the doctor. "I'm going to have to investigate and it will take some time. You stay here with Dayne and I'll take Rubio with me. Don't give him any more and stay off the needle yourself. He won't get loose but you stay awake just the same."

After they had gone Dayne sat up and tossed the hair out of her face. It was marked but I was relieved to see that it wasn't turning blue. Her eyes were swollen and red from weeping. I raised my head. "Acting under orders," I croaked.

"Hey, you awake?" asked the doctor, having been half asleep himself. He heaved himself straight in his chair. "How do you feel?"

"Without these ropes I think I could break every bone in your wormy old carcass."

"Doubtless, doubtless." He chuckled. "I was a bucko like you once."

"What got you, snow or H.?"

He flushed. "How'd you like to get kicked where you kicked Rubio?"

"Cut me loose and let's have a kicking bee."

"I may be old," he said puffing, "but I'm no fool."

"Maybe. This place'll be too hot to hold you come morning."

He smacked his lips and composed himself in his chair again, his lids drooping drowsily.

I cut a glance at Dayne again. Her eyes were wide and begging but she didn't say anything.

"Acting under orders," I sneered again. She went pale and the blotches stood out.

Her lips went into action saying, "Please, please, please," then I remembered that she had told me to go, go, go and I hadn't gone. Now I was here. Maybe there was more to this than I knew. A man is always willing to give a beautiful woman practically any break she doesn't deserve. I grinned at her. "Sorry," I said with my lips. Her gratitude was pathetic, her eyes aswim again with tears, and made me feel like a dog. That, of course, is the way it's supposed to work. I tested the cord that held me and found it to be well tied and strong. I would never break it. The chair, however, was another matter. It was rickety and should fall apart without too much trouble. While the old man dozed, I rocked back and forth in the chair, utilizing the play in the joints. Soon I was rewarded by a rung popping loose with a dull note. The doctor didn't wake. I glanced at Dayne and her face was again taken over with fear. She was so scared she didn't know where she was. I whispered to her to come untie me but she didn't seem to hear. I worked until I had the chair about ready to fall apart; then I lunged as much as I could, mostly fell forward into the doctor, carrying him over backward in his ancient armchair. He yelled hoarsely and between him fighting to get me off him and me wrenching myself into a mass of dislocations the cheap chair just fell apart and I managed to stand up. My arms were still entangled with chair parts, so as he stood up I jumped and planted both feet right in his kisser as hard as I could. He went backward and out, his face flat and beginning to turn blue. In a few seconds I managed to get free of the cords. I looked for my gun but it wasn't around.

"Where's my pistol?" I asked, turning to the couch, but she wasn't around either. Gone, disappeared, vamoosed. "Scared to death," I muttered and started for the door. I heard sounds and snapped the lights off.

I opened the door and saw in the dim light a hallway with a set of stairs leading directly away from the door and at the bottom moving up were Raspy and Rubio. They were prodding someone ahead of them. So I stood aside in the dark and let them come until Raspy passed me. I reached out and twisted his gun aside just as it went off. I could feel the warm wet debris as it spattered but I was too busy to worry about that. I conked Rubio just as he was swinging his weapon into action. They fell backward down the stairs with me and my captive right behind them. He was a slim little twirp and I muscled him out of the place ahead of me until the street light could shine on him. A whistle shrilled in the distance and pounding feet were coming nearer. A blue coat came foaming up under a full head of steam and to save any argument I flashed my identification on him and watched him simmer down.

"There's an off-color M.D. upstairs," I told him. "He may live. There's one guy who's a corpse and a third one at the foot of the stairs there whom I tapped on the onion. This I'm taking with me. If your outfit needs me I'll be available, but right now time's awastin'."

I hailed a cab and threw my boy into it and off we took.

"Well, Robert, what's the deal?"

He squirmed and began to weep. "I don't know nothing, I don't—"

"Come off it and talk. Know where we're going? To the office, so keep a closed lip if you want to."

"I'll get fired," he whimpered, "I'll get fired, get fired as sure as anything."

"Oh, fudge!" I growled. "Keep your lace handkerchief misery to yourself." I felt a gory hole in the back of my head. "I got my own troubles."

We stopped at DuPont Circle and I had the cabby call Frank Barber who promised to be at the office when we arrived. He was, and in an ugly mood. He took one look at me and snarled. "Didn't I tell you to call me?"

"I was intelephon-communicado, but look what I picked up. Mister or Miss Hitchens declines comment."

Frank turned to Robert. "Well, what the hell is this?"

"Maybe I'd better tell it short-like," I said. "I told you about the gal. I went around early tonight and was just in time to take a guy that was slapping her around and I got taken by another from behind. I woke up all full of sleep and they were asking me questions that I couldn't answer. Later when they were convinced I was telling the truth two of them left and I stayed behind with a doctor they were using and the girl. I managed to shake the chair I was sitting in to pieces and flopped on the doc who was asleep. I got loose and plastered him. When I got ready to go they were coming back up the stairs with this." I jerked a finger at Robert who had sunk into a chair and was looking very wan and hopeless.

"When they left," I continued, "the leader was wondering if he had been given the wrong dope, implied that it would be too bad for the informer if the info wasn't straight. He came back with Robert here. What did you tell them, Robert?"

"Yeah," bellowed Frank, turning beet red, "what did you tell 'em?" He picked up a pair of handcuffs and slashed Robert across the face with them. The old cop had come out in him again.

Robert fell back and began to cry, mopping a cut lip with a snowy handkerchief, looking at the blood and shivering.

Frank drew back again. "Talk!" he roared.

Robert nodded and shrank away from him. "All right. I'll talk and maybe get killed if I do."

"Either way," I said, "so you might heed nearest danger."

"He made me tell."

"Who made you tell what?" asked Frank.

"He wanted to know if any of our staff were ever called over to the main office. I said Mr. Markham was."

Frank looked momentarily baffled and I fell into a chair laughing. "Oh, boy, this is rich."

"I'm glad," snarled Frank. "Tell me too, so I can laugh."

"Robert read the memo wrong. I'm to go tomorrow. When did you tell him I went, Robert?"

He was green now and his jaw slack. "Yesterday. Didn't you go yesterday—Thursday?"

Frank purpled. "You blithering ass, today is Thursday and he's not to go until tomorrow."

"Hey," I said coming out of the chair, "that wasn't smart."

"Nothing lost," he said calmly. "Where he'll be one day'll be just like another except longer maybe. Now who is "he"?"

"I don't know, I don't know. Really, I don't."

"How'd you meet him?"

"We have a club," Robert gasped, his face going another shade of bluish white "At the club."

"And what could he have used on you to make you take important secrets out of this office?"

Robert fainted but Frank caught him before he fell to the floor. He shoved him back in the chair and slapped him a couple of times. Finally he opened his eyes. "Did I tell you?" he whispered.

"No," said Frank, "and you'd better be fast about it."

It took some time, however, for him to get it out. Finally he said. "He knew my boyfriend."

"And who's the boyfriend?"

"Please, Mr. Barber, don't make me tell that. I—He—"

"Talk," roared Frank picking up the handcuffs again and slapping a thick palm with them.

Robert gulped and shuddered from sheer funk, then blurted. "Allan Cranston. He had taken pictures of us."

"God damn!" Frank went to the desk and sat down. "How in the tattertailed hell do creeps like Robert and Cranston ever get in places like this? I'll be damned if I don't feel like agreeing with the Republicans sometimes."

I nodded, unable to find anything to say. I didn't doubt the boy because it took too much out of him to tell it. He hung in his chair partly conscious, his beardless face as blank as a sheet of paper, his sensitive, too curved lips a dirty fuscia.

"What'll you do?" I asked.

"I'm going to bust this thing wide open," Frank said truculently, "that's what I'm going to do." He stood up and pounded the desk. "Now I'm not bored any more."

CHAPTER THREE

THE NEXT MORNING from nine forty-five till ten I waited in an outer office which held a chick with nice legs and a chest that was as rocky as pineapple cheese. It didn't jiggle as much as a hair. False! I can spot 'em.

At the stroke of ten she nodded to me. "You may go in, Mr. Markham."

I don't know where they came from but the Cheese's office was loaded. As usual, his rugged personality had things in hand even though the conversation was broken up into knots, business not yet having been started.

The big guy shook my hand. "Glad to have you in, Markham," he said, his granite face softened by a smile. "Good job you did for us."

"Thanks. I had some luck."

"Your modesty isn't what brought you here," he said a trifle grimly.

"Just why am I here? I see some pretty famous faces. You running short of men?"

"No. This is to be a special assignment."

"Norcross in on it or is he just slumming?"

"Norcross is in on it."

I grinned. "Then you might as well send the rest of us home."

"Wait until you've heard all the dope, then judge. I need a lot of men like him."

Norcross is a fabulous figure. He has that necessary quotient of indestructibility, a steel trap mind and a cold ruthlessness

that is famous. Leading a band of Chetniks during the other fracas, he wiped out an entire German airstrip to the last man and
burned all planes. They ambushed arriving help and wiped them
out. Norcross took the one long barrack as his own after they had
gotten the sentries. He threw four grenades in at one end, raced
to the other and mowed down foes with a sub-gun as they came
out. There must be a hundred tales of his audacity, cunning and
resourcefulness. Nominally, he's a colonel in the Marines, but he
stays on loan all the time to this or that service or bureau.

At the moment he was leaning against a window facing, talking to the most puzzling hunk of man I ever saw. He was swarthy
dark with a face diabolically pointed, his features regular almost
to prettiness but with a cast of hard purpose that balanced the
prettiness. He was dressed in a uniform that fitted with a certain
piratical carelessness and an elegance that no country affords
in their issue stuff. Plainly, this rig had been carefully tailored
to order of the very finest available materials and the cordovan
riding boots, something you rarely see any more, must have
stood him a cool hundred bucks; and their gloss was a wonder
to behold.

Norcross was lank as a crane but he looked like a coiled
spring even in repose. His shoulders were tremendous and his
waist as narrow as a dancer's. His face looked like it had been
hacked out of old fire-hardened wood in sudden flat planes and
angles and his eyes were chips of blue ice. An executioner on the
side of the law.

The Cheese walked around to his desk and struck it once with
the palm of his hand. "Your attention, gentlemen." Conversation
faded instantly. There was discipline in this room. Even an angry
purple-faced admiral almost snapped to. The services were represented, all right, and the only one who looked at all happy was
General O'Rourke of the Marines. "Red Mike," we used to call
him. He was a little amused at the Admiral who appeared on
the verge of apoplexy from pure rage. General Stafford of the Air

Corps looked harassed and nervous and General Gordon Haspel of Army looked pompous and incompetent. He was both—as he was later snatched up for talking too much and saying too little.

"Gentlemen," said the big fellow again, "we're gathered here on a matter of the gravest importance and frankly I wish it hadn't been handed to me. Ever since the end of the war we've been fed on suspicions and whatnot as to what happened to many of the leaders of Germany. Most if not all of it is the sheerest fiction. However, something has come up that reminds us of this fiction rather sharply. I do not imply that there is any mastermind behind it. They have excellent organization and their feelers reach into many far flung places. As all of you know, our enemies would like nothing better than to throw our economy into a descending spiral. Better still would be a panic that would take away even the relatively softer spiral. In other words, something that would cause an abrupt and cataclysmic blow to our economic structure. As fantastic as any such coup sounds, events have occurred that makes it a threat if not an actuality. There have been incidents that sound like something from a fantasy story. However, I think I will allow the folks who know first hand to tell their stories. Gentlemen, allow me to present Sir Geoffry Travestock."

A tall tanned Britisher of possibly forty years stood up and bowed slightly. "My story is simple. I am connected with the British Government and my connection has to do with the diamond industry. One of our problems we dub as I.D.B., which means illicit diamond buying. It once was a thriving bit of lawlessness but it is under control now. In Africa recently, I'm not at liberty to reveal the locality, a strike was made that was fabulous in that a tremendous number of stones were found in a relatively small area and quickly. They were gathered by hand labor and stored in a well-guarded hut until they could be transported by truck to the company's main office.

"At the same time a large number of stones from another and still remote locality arrived and was included in the shipment.

These trucks were ambushed at night and every stone taken. Men were killed and the king's ransom in diamonds stolen. Not a week later a steamer out of Cape Town with a huge cargo of gems steamed northward bound for Antwerp. Off Sierra Leone she was stopped and all diamonds taken off."

Norcross, his teakwood face unchanged, leaned forward. "Stopped by what, Sir Geoffry?"

Sir Geoffry took a deep breath and clasped his hands in front of him. "By a submarine of the Snorkel type that put a shell into her afterbridge structure when she refused to stop as ordered."

The silence was thick for a moment. He continued. "I need not tell you gentlemen what the effect would be should these stones be dumped on the market suddenly."

"Couldn't buyers be made liable if they bought them?" asked General Stafford.

Sir Geoffry smiled tolerantly. "That is not easily done. Unfortunately, neither Britain nor the United States is so widely liked that we could achieve much by such a request. Naturally the legitimate buyers of Belgium and the Netherlands are most anxious to cooperate but if the gems start pouring into the market cut and polished by those whose purpose is to cause a panic in the market, even the legitimate buyers will have to look to their own protection.

"There are always people whose ambition it is to acquire a large gem at low cost. We have managed, through strict control, to keep the prices stable, but this could ruin everything.

"Manufacturers who use the inferior diamond—that is, one not of the quality to be made into ornamental baubles—are our biggest customers. They are the backbone of the industry and who among them would balk at acquiring his diamonds at half the usual cost or less? No, gentlemen, it is not a simple matter and the diamond industry is quivering in its boots. And as if this were not enough, a certain venerable Indian Prince whose diamonds are said to be the most fabulous in any private collection and certainly the largest in the world has been robbed just as our motor train was robbed in Africa, by bandits using a helicopter at night. He was surprised, overpowered and his vaults cleaned. A large amount of gold was taken also. So we see that two parcels which would have been stored and used as the demand indicated and another that might be larger than these two and certainly more valuable since it contains all gem diamonds, stand to be thrown on the open market by one method or another. People who would kill to get them there would certainly not be deterred by the finer points of ethics in their disposal, especially when there is the possibility that sheer panic is their goal." He sat down and there was another silence.

"Captain Soldarez." My enigmatic Latin swept the assembly with agate eyes that seemed to have laughter and frolic in their depths—if you could see past the tigerish gleam first noted.

"I am a neighbor from the south," he said in a gentle liquid voice. He looked about for a moment. "To all who know what I mean, I carry a white card. To those who do not, it will mean nothing." I could sense that several, including Norcross, knew what he meant but aside from a momentary flicker of an eye or the casual raising of a head there was no sign that any had heard him. To the rest of us he was talking Greek. "A very singular occurrence happened some years ago in my country concerning which I shall have to mimic Sir Geoffry in that I can only suggest what I mean. I cannot be specific.

"In lieu of an explanation envision for a moment a volcano erupting suddenly and miles away, down a gorge, a town of some ten thousand souls seeing the imminent ruin of their life's work.

"Luckily, there was an engineer in the town at the time and after an inspection he saw that a narrow point of the gorge a cliff could be toppled into the chasm by high explosives and might possibly arrest the flow of lava. He was commissioned to the job which was very successful.

"The eruption ceased, the lava cooled and the town was saved. The action of the lava might make one think that it was sorry for all the anxiety it had caused because as it lay trapped in the chasm an unbelievable thing happened. The terrific heat smelted out a precious metal which trickled down from the area of the dam and collected in several pools. It was the work of hundreds of miners taking years of toil and effort done in a matter of hours. Some years passed before a peon found it and assumed it to be lead which he intended to take home and use. Naturally, when he discovered it was gold he took the discovery to the *Alcalde* of the town and the government became interested. Now, as you know, your country has for years been our best customer for metals of all sorts and gold in particular. The amount so smelted would have had the same effect on the gold market that the diamonds Sir Geoffry mentioned would have on the diamond market and, by the same token, there was no way this gold could be prevented from falling into the wrong hands. As long as we held the bulk of it and sent it in to the regular markets in the proper amounts all was well. But such was not to be the case. It is not yet certain how the debacle occurred; but assuredly it is known that enough gold went out in two shipments to cause serious damage to the world gold market. In fact, there is evidence that such has already happened. Again it was a Snorkel-type submarine that stopped our small freighter in the Gulf of Mexico and threw three shells into her before she would halt. She had a five-year quota of gold aboard, at the usual rate of delivery an almost incalculable fortune, right? There are spots in the world where tremendous amounts of gold can be disposed of at good prices and in these days of depreciated currencies I think I need dwell on that particular angle of the case no longer."

"One moment," said a man who looked like a Wall Street financier. "I know something of gold mining. I question the possibility of such a tremendous array of perfect conditions that could melt gold out of a vein and deposit it in the pure state in a puddle waiting for someone to discover it."

Soldarez's smile was thin and had a steely quality about it. "It is possible that you are right."

"Then what do you mean by all this folderol?"

"My good fellow," said the Captain with condescending patience, "since I did not, at the beginning, promise to tell the exact truth about this matter for reasons which do not here concern us, your remarks only interrupt, they do not help. What I have just described could be within the realm of possibility. On the other hand, we might have discovered the gold of the Lost Atlantis beneath some Mayan ruin at Chichen Itza. The means by which the gold was discovered is not what we are here to discuss and I think, sir, if you and others will allow the proceedings to go forward without such interference we will be through more quickly."

"There can be no disagreement with that," said the Cheese, nodding to Soldarez to continue.

He shrugged eloquently. "I was about through and I think there is another gentleman who has something to say about gold."

A well-dressed man with dark sun-and wind-burned skin got up and nodded to the assembly. "I'm from one of our northwestern gold-producing areas. Though it hasn't been publicized we've lost three shipments of gold through cleverly planned robbery and until we were contacted regarding this overall business we thought it just someone robbing for the gold alone, although I must admit that it hasn't gone well with our stockholders who face a long period of lean dividends. Actually it would cause a considerable disturbance if just this amount of gold were to be employed against a currency. I hope that this meeting will devise some ways of preventing what is threatened." He smiled wryly. "And we'd like to have our gold back, too."

There was a general titter of laughter at that sally and the Cheese nodded. "Recovery will be high on the preferred list," he said. "Those robberies you spoke of, Mr. Jorkyn, naturally came under our notice and we worked hard and fruitlessly on them. Unfortunately a helicopter doesn't leave much in the way of clues."

Norcross leaned forward. "Helicopter, again?"

Jorkyn nodded. "After all, such an aircraft is no longer a curiosity and I'm not as concerned about it as I am about how they knew when each quantity of gold would be assembled at one poorly guarded place. It was a secret to all but a very few men whom we trust implicitly."

"Money talks." I sat up surprised. I had been the speaker. I turned red and felt like a fool. "Pardon the interruption," I said and hung my head.

The Cheese laughed. "Mr. Markham spoke unconsciously. He's been working on a case for us where a foreign government was buying employees in some departments. They invariably chose those who were in financial straits or who had been affluent at some time in the past and had come on hard times. Markham stopped the practice before it became serious."

He stood up. "There are other stories like the ones you've just heard but I think we have seen the pattern."

Sir Geoffry said, "I might mention that although it was not in my department, there have been robberies of gold in South Africa."

The Cheese nodded. "We know of those, too. The point is this—are we in agreement that we must concede that these robberies are being carried out by a group under certain shrewd and capable leadership for some purpose other than self-enrichment or piracy for personal gain?"

There seemed to be pretty good agreement and everyone was concerned except the military men, who were plainly irked by the whole proceedings. Maybe they figured they would get theirs no matter what happened to the economies of their countries.

"Sir Geoffry," asked the bureau head, "have you been briefed by your government?"

"I spent a fast hour at the Home Office," said Sir Geoffry. "I was told to give you any assistance or information you desired." He smiled quizzically. "I brought Eric Vaarden and John Oldwick as you requested, although they are not inclined to share any secrets with me."

The Cheese nodded soberly. "They came without question so you can be assured that they are known to us." He turned to Admiral Grieve. "Your research department lost a snorkel submarine, did it not?"

The Admiral went purple again. "It did, sir."

"And the coup was carried out at night with the attackers arriving by helicopter just when the craft was being readied for a test cruise?"

"You seem to have all the facts." The Admiral wasn't pleased to admit it, either. Someone in his security setup would catch it.

"General O'Rourke, you lost quite a lot of small arms ammunition, did you not?"

Red Mike wasn't sad. He grinned bigger than ever. "That we did. Caught us shorthanded during a holiday and lifted a modest amount of fifty-caliber and small arms stuff. Naturally, we don't mount guard with the thought of enemy helicopters here within our own borders."

"Naturally not. You, General Stafford, lost a tiny fighter designed to be carried beneath the belly of a bomber, did you not?"

"Not in the sense that the submarine and ammunition were lost. Both the pilot and plane disappeared while testing."

"No reports on either pilot or plane?"

"No, sir."

"Is it not true, General, that the pilot who normally would have flown the craft was not aboard it?"

General Stafford caught his breath and began to turn red. Ah, I thought, the Cheese had been reading someone else's mail.

"That," replied the General slowly, "is true."

The big boy turned to the Admiral again. "Was the submarine equipped to carry a small plane?"

"Yes," said Grieve, "but if you're connecting these two incidents I might point out that a jet plane must have a great deal more take-off room than a conventional propeller-driven craft."

"Yes," said Stafford eagerly, "that's true."

The powerful face lighted with a smile. "I understand that RATO is sometimes helpful. So is a catapult." That got them but why they thought he didn't know from nothing about such things is beyond me. That guy knows something about everything.

"And I," said General Haspel, unable to wait his turn, "lost a few containers of Lewisite. You don't expect them to start a gas war, do you?"

"You lost twenty-four cylinders of Lewisite," said the chief. "As to their object in taking any such unlikely thing, I confess I'm in the dark. Do you have any suggestions?"

General Haspel had a lot of throaty noises to make but no suggestions. The chief stood up. "You gentlemen of the military may go. I did not get you here to poke fun at you but so these gentlemen might see in a dramatic way just what we have to face. Thank you for your cooperation."

He smiled politely. But not one of them had anything to say as they filed out—except Red Mike. He stopped at the door and grinned. "Give 'em hell, Sam."

The chief gave him a wave and the door closed. He turned to Sir Geoffry. "I'll expect your government to give Vaarden and Oldwick every possible support in their sphere of operations."

"I can guarantee that, sir."

"Good. Captain Soldarez, I assume you will have the cooperation of your government. I know your president well and I understand you and he are close friends."

"That is right, sir. My government will give every possible assistance."

"Good. Now, gentlemen, there are a few things I'd like to discuss with my white card men. The rest of you may go. Not you, Markham. I want you here, too."

I sat back down and looked over the ten men that remained. Not a single one of them could have been called ordinary. Vaarden was a blond Dutchman with the keenest amber eyes I ever saw. Oldwick was one of those crisp silent Englishmen with that overpowering aura of capability the type sends off. And there was Norcross and Soldarez. The rest I didn't know.

CHAPTER FOUR

THE CHIEF looked us over affectionately. "Gentlemen, allow me to compliment myself for picking you."

Soldarez grinned like Satan. "It is to us you have delivered the compliment, sir. I'd rather have my card than my life."

There were other kind things said and all the time I was getting curiouser and curiouser. "I applaud all this kind talk," I said, "and maybe I'm better off than I know, but the only white card I have was given me by Mike, a bartender friend of mine. It has a dirty verse on the back of it."

The chief smote his forehead as though crushed by some gross oversight and delved into a strong metal box in a drawer. In a moment he handed me a wallet-sized plastic card with my name engraved on it.

"The explanation will come later, Markham, but you heard what Soldarez Said about it. Now to business. Norcross, you've had the most experience, I think. Do you have any suggestions?"

The cold-eyed man nodded. "I've been thinking. These people need support and by that I mean they must have a good many men, men whose trustworthiness is beyond question. They are probably clever beyond the normal expectancy. They must have some sort of home base. As I see it, we are totally without evidence as to where this base is located. We have none of their people and as far as I can see we have little chance of getting any."

"If the pollywog may speak," I said with fitting humility, "we do have one. Maybe two." Brother, did I get their attention.

"Come, Markham," said the chief testily, "don't play coy. What are you talking about?"

I explained my adventures of last night. "The girl will naturally have vanished except that chicks of her caliber can't evaporate without leaving someone who saw them evaporate. This lug that I knocked down the stairs is probably pretty uncomfortable right now, but he should be able to talk. Especially if we used a little sodium amytal on him as they did on me last night. The doctor might know something, but I doubt it. I think he was just used. Now some of you smart people tell me one thing. How come me to be picked out? True, they got their timing wrong due to the stupidity of an informer, but if they caught me now and loaded me like they did last night the enemy would be tipped."

I looked my question around but the only one who reacted at all was Norcross. A frosty little smile wrinkled the corners of his mouth. "Are you the Markham who shacked up with a rather high chief's daughter on Luzon and had half the Philippine constabulary looking for you?"

I was so damned embarrassed that I almost wept. My face burned like a jet fighter's tail.

A landslide of laughter came down on me, even the Frenchman and two Chinese joining in the fun. The big cotton-headed Scowegian just grinned and Oldwick let loose one vulgar "Haw" and shut up as though ashamed that he had laughed.

"It occurs to me," said Norcross, still smiling, "that they picked you because you're younger than the rest of us and it has been pretty well established that you have a weakness for pretty—faces."

When I finally managed to get over that blow I still had another question. "You could be right at that, but now I want to know—did you guys select me for the same reason?"

The chief cut me short. "I'll allow Captain Soldarez to explain that, Markham. Right now we want to find out a few things about this man who is still living."

We tried hard, but there wasn't much he could tell. Either I had tapped him with a little too much vim or the nose dive down the steps had cracked his head. He rambled and mumbled answers that didn't make any sense but there was one consistency to his raving. The word "Sierra."

Later we had another caucus and Soldarez lifted a shoulder and said, "Sierra, as you all probably know, is Spanish for mountain. But that leaves us as badly off as ever."

"It seems hopeless," said the chief with a sigh. "All I can do is to dispatch you to your own areas and hope something will happen in one of them. I suggest that you use your recruiting powers to whatever extent you see fit. If you need arms your governments will supply them and should it be necessary you will be able to call on bulk reinforcements. Keep in touch with this office and I'll act liaison for all of you. Soldarez, are you ready to depart?"

"Yes, sir, as soon as Markham and I have nosed about for the girl. If she's still in Washington we might be able to use her. I do not agree with Markham that she is a mere tool, but I certainly understand why he feels that way if she's half as attractive as he seems to think."

That was it and before many minutes had passed, this flawless Latin and myself were facing Mike across the walnut bar of the Iron Horse.

"You're a man after my own heart, Señor Markham," said Soldarez, running a thumbnail quickly under the slimly elegant black moustache that was so perfect it suggested falseness. "After all, the world will not tumble in a moment and there is always *mañana*. At the moment I should like a scotch and soda as big as the tallest glass in the house will accommodate."

"Whatcha want big?" asked Mike, "the scotch or the soda?"

"Let there be harmony between them. In other words, treat them as equals."

"Arf and arf comin' up in a mo'," said Mike who had been to England.

I had the usual B and B and when Soldarez had smacked his delicate lips the second time he asked, "What are you doing by way of security? By that I mean to prevent a repetition of your initial kidnaping."

"Well, for one thing, I won't go sticking my crumpet in the way of any more saps." I patted myself over the automatic I carried. "Out in the open they got this to contend with."

"Ah, yes. I think I heard something about you upsetting an attempt on your life rather neatly."

"Well enough, I guess. I can shoot a pistol. They couldn't. There's a lot like them. With a rifle or a shotgun a tyro can be dangerous but a pistol doesn't have enough pointing quotient and is given to bucking around a lot. I learned to shoot with a Colt Peacemaker and it had a muzzle blast that'd scalp you and a kick like a sore cow. That's why this automatic seems as smooth as silk with a trigger pull a kitten could actuate. Without boasting, I can shoot it."

"I think you're a little curious about this, aren't you? Your part, I mean."

"Yeah, and I'm curious about this card I'm carrying."

"You'll be prouder of that than you were of the first pistol you ever owned. You were chosen, all right, but this gold piracy had nothing to do with it."

"What do you mean?"

"You were chosen like the rest of us after the most painstaking screening job ever done on a man. Every point of your personality went through the mill and was scrutinized. It was all studied by a top clinical psychologist and a report made on your temperament, stability, the whole works. Your school teachers were quizzed, your coaches, fellow ball players, representatives from all your activities who associated with you over any substantial period. Your inclusion in this matter is fortuitous. I've been a white card man since 1947 and these are the first orders I've had."

"All the rest are white card men?"

"They are. Of that last group, I mean. The chief has men in every country in the world."

"What did he mean about your recruiting powers?"

"Popularity is a point considered when a man is investigated. In addition to that he must be a practical student of character. In the event of some cataclysmic occurrence like the falling of a country—well, such as the United States, and I pray it never happens—these men would be the hard core of a resistance movement. They would be required to recruit men who would in turn recruit others; a self-energizing sort of thing."

I felt a little uplifted. "Say, I could raise quite a force myself."

"That's the idea. And from this force would spring other forces when your men picked theirs and so on. The idea is both unique and inspired. This will be the first test and lucky you, you're in on it."

I tapped the bar for more of the same and Soldarez also repeated. My new friend could pour it down.

All of a sudden I had a warm feeling for this dandy, this superbly suave man. "My friends call me Ches," I said, grinning and holding out my hand.

His grin was like a light going on. "To mine I'm Phillipe or just plain Phil. My mother was part French and preferred the French spelling."

I took my hand back to see if it was all there. It was but the fingers looked a little white. He may be a dandy, I thought, but he's made of stout metal. I then noticed the long muscles, muscles of a man not only superbly built but in top condition. He was a natural clothes horse with door-wide shoulders and good chest, a waist as slim as Apollo and the hard-trained legs of a track athlete.

While Soldarez loafed that afternoon I went back to my own chief and told him what was up. He was happy about all the things he was lining up, with which he was going to deal a lot of people untold misery and he had Robert still with him, making a talking picture of his confession.

Robert looked as though he had been touched by the kiss of death, but Frank wasn't in a merciful mood. He almost brushed me out and admitted later that he nearly blew a gasket because he thought I had walked out on him. He had forgotten ever giving his permission.

I went back to the Iron Horse at five and found Soldarez seated on his stool, the same one. He and Mike were having at it regarding some obscure question. We had a couple together and Phil made a suggestion. "Let's go to Hogate's and find out how good seafood can be. You'll be my guest, of course."

"Where are you staying?"

"At the Wirden House. Why?"

"I think you'd better put up at my place. From now on, unless we entertain the thin hope that I got 'em all, we're going to be targets. Four eyes are better than two."

He nodded. "I won't bore you with the usual protestations. Your idea is a good one and your description of the hope as thin is also good. I was followed here."

"Followed here?"

"That's right. And I must say the man is a superb trailer. He was so absolutely drab and a part of the scenery that I became suspicious and employed all the tried and true methods of ascertaining his job. If you've ever noticed, it is rare to find a man with no outstanding characteristics. No colored handkerchief in his breast pocket, no feather in his hat. His suit was some appalling shade of grey and if he lost it in a hay patch he'd never find it. In other words, his point of identification was his unique drabness. He never pressed me and most of the time stayed out of sight."

"Now, ain't that ducky? What say we give him the slip."

"How?"

"Out the back. The john opens into an alley that goes through the block and can't be seen from the front. He's outside some place, waiting for you to come out."

"Let's go."

We did and made our way leisurely to the street and hailed a cab. I don't drive to work because traffic jams irk me. We went to the Wirden House and retrieved Phil's luggage which was plentiful and went home to a dinner which made Phil forget that he had wanted to guest me.

Lonzo was a little hostile for a while but he finally unbent and he and Phil made with Spanish that sounded as rapid as machine gun fire. But Lonzo was uneasy even after he thawed out under Phil's good nature. Finally he had an opportunity and whispered in my ear. "There's a very lovely titmouse in your room."

I flinched. "Dammit, didn't I tell you no more—"

"I did not find her. She found you. She came here in the afternoon and there has been a blue car circling the block ever since."

"Well, don't bother about the captain. We're together." I got up as Phil came out of the bath.

"Stand by for a shock," I said, grinning. "I hear I have tender company." I went into the bedroom and saw no one, but the closet door was ajar.

"Come out, come out, wherever you are," I sang blithely.

She came out hesitantly and it was I who got the shock. She was attired in a powder blue creation as simple as a sack but fitting like no sack ever had. I felt a hot flash go through me.

"Dayne."

Her lips trembled and she wrung her slim hands together. "Ches, I'm so sorry about last night. I had to come."

I stepped forward and took her cold hands in mine. "Forget about last night. You look scared to death."

Her breath shuddered as she inhaled inwardly. "I am. They'll kill me, Ches."

"Who are they?"

She shook her head and tears came to her eyes. "Please don't make me tell you, please don't make me. They'll kill you, too."

"They tried," I said ruggedly. "Come on out and meet a man who's on our side."

I introduced them and Phil was nearly rocked out of that piratical aplomb of his. He bowed low and made his effort in German that sounded flawless. Dayne paled and answered him. He went further, sounding a lot more flowery and elegant. Whatever he said brought the roses back to her cheeks and she managed a little laugh.

He turned to me. "I had an idea Miss Holcombe might be German, but she isn't. She's Austrian."

I was right. She wasn't a hundred percent American girl. She was Austrian and from here she looked the limit of whatever percentage Austrians run.

"I'm half Austrian," she said. "My father is English." Her voice dropped and her eyes looked fresh misery. "If he's alive."

We sat and watched her eat a little, then we cornered her and put her through a quiz session that was a wing ding. She answered everything she could but she didn't know much.

"My father was a manufacturing jeweler in Vienna and, like a great many of the middle class artisans, he had his troubles. Then he disappeared and I didn't hear from him for a month. I was singing in a café at the time and when a man appeared telling me that my father wanted me I was overjoyed. I went with this man and that was the last I ever saw of Vienna. I've never seen my father either. I was taken to Casablanca where I met a huge fat man who told me if I'd work for him and take orders I'd see my father again. If I didn't I'd never see him alive." Her eyes swam in tears for a moment. She dabbed them with a tiny handkerchief. "What could I do but take orders? What could I do when they told me to make your acquaintance, Ches?"

"Never mind that now. Who is the leader in Washington?"

"The man you saw last night."

"Rubio's boss?"

"Yes."

I looked at Phil and he looked at me. I said, "I hate to disagree with you, Dayne, but there are others."

She shrugged. "I suppose so. The man you saw was Karl Kroning. Ever since I left Casablanca I've been with him and Rubio. There have been others who came and talked with them but Kroning always seemed to be the leader."

"What made them want to get me?"

"A man in your department whom they had blackmailed told Karl that you had been interviewed by a very important person about a very important assignment that was pending. Karl wanted to know what it was."

"His informant had made a mistake. I hadn't been interviewed yet. Were they interested in any others besides me?"

"They mentioned a gentleman by the name of Norcross."

Phil nodded. "I should think so. He isn't exactly unknown. Any others."

She frowned. "Maybe this will help. While we were still in Casablanca something happened that made the fat man very pleased. Then he heard that an Englishman, I think his name was Travestock, had left for the United States. I was present when he talked to Karl about it. He said, "Now is the time for you to show your claws, Karl. Take the little one with you. She will be of great help since all Americans are fools where a woman is concerned. Don't trust her too far but she dare not disobey you. If she does she will receive a part of her father through the mails."

She broke down and cried for a while and the swarthy man across from me watched her through murderous black eyes. "I think," he said softly, "that I'm going to enjoy this assignment."

"Why did you leave them, Dayne?" I asked. "Aren't you still afraid for your father?"

She nodded and dabbed at her eyes. "I went back to the place where Karl stays and no one ever came."

"He's dead," I said flatly.

She gasped, her face lighted for a second, then fell again. "If there are others, what difference will it make?"

"Why did you come here?"

Her face was a study in hopelessness. "I thought you might help me, Ches. You seemed nice. You seemed to like me." Her chin trembled. "I didn't have any place to go. They never gave me much money. I just didn't know what else to do."

"How did you know where I lived?"

"They had a lot of information about you. I don't know where they got it."

"I can guess. Friend Robert, no doubt." I bit my lip for a moment, not knowing what to do with her.

"If you're wondering," said Phil, "I have a suggestion." "I have a suggestion."

"I'm wide open," I said.

"Take her to a hotel, a good one. Put her up in a room openly, under her own name. Let her be watched constantly for visitors. Any attempt to get in touch with her will produce another one for us to question."

"Sounds good. I'll call the Cheese."

I did and he liked the idea. He also gave me the dope on the M.D. He was an ex-doctor who had lost his license for some felony and picked up a living how and when he could. They had him in the cooler awaiting his confession; since he was on the needle it wouldn't be long but the Cheese didn't think he knew much. I didn't either.

"What do you think of this idea, Dayne?"

Her eyes were wells of hopelessness. "What does it matter?"

"What about your father—I mean with you running away from them like this?"

"Ches, I can't think any more. If he's worth anything to them they'll keep him. If he's not, then he's already dead."

"A very intelligent conclusion," applauded Phil. "Dayne, I think you're a very brave little girl."

Her smile was a travesty. "I'm not brave, really. I'm at the end of my rope. I just don't know what to do."

I had a lot I could have said to that but I didn't because Phil was there. "Well, let's be on our way. We'll put you up at the Wirden House."

She gasped. "That's where we were staying."

"Then that makes it better. Are your quarters still paid for?"

"No. There was a notice in the room this morning. You see, they stay in a place and don't pay. Then they move out and leave the bill owed. In that way they cut expenses."

"I see." I went to the phone and called the Wirden House and found them in something of a dither about the suite. I calmed them, promised payment and reinstated Dayne in her old quarters. "Now let's go," I said. "I'll run you over in my car."

She put her hand on my arm. "I know I don't deserve nice treatment from you, Ches, but please believe me when I say I think you are a very gallant gentleman. You must be to be even civil to me after what happened."

"Forget it," I said more roughly than I meant to.

We started out but Phil stopped us. "One moment. Don't you think we'd better go double?"

He grinned at my flush. "Yes," I said. "I must be nuts."

"Understandably," he said. "Now, you two go ahead as though you suspected nothing. I'll follow at a discreet distance."

That was one night I appreciated my neighbor from south of the border. We went on down the two flights and out into the street but Soldarez didn't follow. He hung back in the gloom of the doorway.

Hardly had I pulled open the door of the car when a blue coupe detached itself from a line of parked cars on the other side of the street and zoomed toward us. A burp gun stunned the night air but it died even as it had begun. Soldarez, having been on the watch, unlimbered on the car before it had gotten straight and the gunner died over his piece with only one short burst to his credit. A front tire went out with a .38 caliber bullet through it and the car slewed sideways, giving Phil a momentary broadside glimpse of the driver. That was enough. The automatic barked wickedly twice and a back tire went out. The car slammed into the curb and tried to climb a fireplug, succeeding enough to stall the engine.

CHAPTER FIVE

THE STREET was now alive with noise. Windows went up, women screamed, men asked what the hell in loud frightened voices and two blocks away a whistle pealed shrilly. The usual crowd gathered after the shooting stopped and by the time the cops got there they had quite an audience.

One woman caught Phil by the sleeve. "It was him," she shrilled. "I saw him—I saw him! He shot those poor men in the car and they were just driving by!"

"Ah, shut up," said one cop who had recognized me.

"But I tell you I saw him do it!"

"I beg your pardon," said Phil as gently as a priest, "but if you do not unhand me and cease this screeching I'll murder you some night while you're asleep."

She went white and beat it but I'll bet she enjoyed it for years to come. She could silence any gossip by relating the time when she was threatened with murder—by a murderer.

The driver of the car was still alive but I didn't think he would talk much and he didn't. He died in the same hospital that held Rubio and Rubio preceded him by an hour.

A bullet had burned Dayne's cheek so it seemed it was she whom they were shooting at. How they missed her I'll never know because even a short burst from a Schmeisser is a lot of lead.

All the way to the hotel she sat hunched and forlorn between us. Every now and then she would finger the band-aid over the spot on her cheek where the bullet had burned her.

"They'll get me, Ches, I know they will."

"Not a chance," I said heartily, although I didn't feel that way. "You'll have the protection of the finest police force in the world."

"They'll get me," she whispered.

"What she needs," said Phil, "is a drink."

"That's right. I'll get a bottle and she can have a couple before she goes to sleep."

"Please, Ches, won't you stay with me tonight?—Please, just once."

I could feel Phil's devilish eyes boring into me. I hesitated.

"It's all right," she said dully. "I have no right to ask you, really."

I stopped and bought her a small bottle of good brandy and myself a bottle of bourbon. When we got to the hotel we parked in front where the big canopy came out to meet us in bright light. I helped her out and said to Phil. "Take the car back. I'll stay with her tonight."

He nodded and did me the favor of not grinning at me.

I took her up after receiving the most profuse thanks of the manager and assurance of top service. I told him enough of what was up so he wouldn't send the house dick to tell me to go home. It was a big two-bedroom, living room, kitchenette suite but right now with Dayne in it there was a wonderful sort of light springing from the walls and wild strange music flowing from nowhere.

She sat in a big chair and fell back, her eyes closing and tears starting from beneath the lids. I stood there aching like a hollow tooth and feeling futile.

I didn't feel that way long. I went into the little kitchenette and built both of us tall drinks, brought them back and put them on an end table at one side of the big fawn leather couch.

"Come drink one of Dr. Markham's potions," I said lightly.

She got up, came to me and fell forward in my arms, clutching me as though she were a drowning woman. She wept stormily for a moment then stopped and raised her head. "Now I've spoiled your nice suit and acted like a baby."

I pulled her to me and took from her damp warm lips the sweetest salty kiss I ever tasted. She was taut for a moment but then a gurgle of some deep-seated relief sounded in her throat and she welded herself to me; the flashing tip of her tongue was like a hot dart that pierced my lips and almost made me lose my balance. Finally she drew away, her eyes smoky with emotion and her lips parted and trembling. "Oh, Ches... Ches, that was so sweet."

"Now you leave me with nothing to say."

Her eyes lighted and she seemed to take life again. "Let me say it, always."

"That's a long time," I said with a lightness I wasn't feeling right then, "but you say it with such music. Drink your drink." Dayne took it and sipped while I optically sought out the delicious curves that swelled her clothes with such heart-stopping delight—the slim round of her waist, the proud eager lift of her breasts and a little spot of bare thigh where her skirt had come up unnoticed. Her legs were tucked under her, inclining her my way, and with the little room between us we were almost touching.

Her violet eyes came up to mine. "I'm not afraid any more, Ches."

I smiled. "Maybe you've something altogether different to be afraid of now."

She wrinkled her nose at me. "No, I'm still not afraid."

Well, I could take that a lot of ways but I waited. She finished her drink and handed me the glass.

"That has such a stimulating burn," she said. "I want more."

I did too, so I fixed them, deliberately slugging hers. She didn't seem to notice and sank her lips into its amber coldness.

She put her drink down and came into my arms again; and again my head reeled with the unbelievable impact of her. Her lips were like warm taffy, soft, clinging, demanding. I stroked the soft hair at the base of her neck, down the column of her throat, over her shoulders and down to the narrowest point of her waist where I caught up the soft skin and squeezed it gently. She writhed against me and delved deeper for a something she couldn't get enough of. Her body grew subtly restless in tiny motions that might have been involuntary. I let a forearm rake the peak of a lush breast and a hard shudder went over her. She drew back, her eyes almost purple, looking at me with wonder and something too deep for me to see.

"Ches…what…I'm not afraid, but tell me this isn't just something…just fun for you."

"It isn't just fun." It must have been the way I said it because she smiled mistily, her lips closed over mine and there was a curious laxness about her, a surrender that I couldn't mistake.

Sequence become swifter and where she had been a fully clothed woman, ravenous and hot with passion, she was now a woman half-clothed, her skin fevered and her eyes burning flakes of amethyst lava. Her breasts were against my face and I had a sensation of smothering between them and then being fed the rarest of all delicacies from their coral tips. Her stomach, for all its soft skin, was ribbed with healthy muscle that was now in action feeding her starved lungs.

Her thighs were searing columns of pink-tan ivory and the further my questing hands roved the more unmanageable she became. She tore herself away for a moment, the rest of her clothes vanished in thin air, and then she seemed to cover me, her heated fragrance stinging my nostrils like a whiff of ether and primordial nature stepped out and met the same in me, closed, and rocked us in the oldest of cradles toward that shattering detonation of blazing joy, then the release, the heart pounding descent into a peace as profound as our ecstacy had been mad.

She now fixed us fresh drinks, flitting about her errand as gracefully as a swallow, filled to the brim with the release and the joy of what we had achieved, still as nude as a pumpkin seed.

She came back with the pony glasses and dipping the tips of each breast in her brandy she offered them to me with a naive sweetness that took most of my breath away. The chill marvels of her offering took the rest of it.

I drank and she drank and we talked and indulged in playful digs and pinchings. We were in the midst of a high class apartment hotel, accepted and safe and wasn't this the United States? Then I found I couldn't see well. I was striving to focus my eyes on her. At first she took on a delicate fuzzy look that was delightful. Then when I tried to brush away the fuzz I couldn't and the delight faded. I tested my vision on various objects and tried to probe through the fog for some constructive solution. I didn't go out like the guy in high fiction does—one drink and down he goes. This took time. I didn't suspect being drugged right then because I couldn't imagine her doing it and there was no one else who could have.

It was only when I could make nothing of the big living room mirror but a shapeless lead-colored blob that I got scared and leaped to my feet. I don't think I stayed there very long because somewhere between the act and the completion, something pulled my switch.

I was riding a cloud, it seemed, but no cloud I ever saw jounced like this one did. After half an hour the cloud turned into the back seat of a jeep and was more uncomfortable than ever.

It was a country road and could have been Maryland or Virginia. It was dark as pitch on either side of the road and a chilly drizzle fell steadily. The windshield wiper smack-smacked with such rhythmic monotony, it soon built up into a drum beat that had my head rocking inside.

I was about to get up and attack those in front when I realized that I was tied with something like a clothesline and from the feel of the stuff it might just as easily have hung me.

My legs were noosed but this time there was no rickety chair to break down to gain slack. I wondered what had happened to the chief's boys who were supposed to be watching the place. I wondered what had happened to Dayne. I hadn't heard her complain about the drink, but I hadn't done any complaining either. The driver was the biggest guy in the shoulders I ever saw and the way he hunched over the wheel gave the impression of brute power. His head was too small and all the rest of him too large. The other fellow was about average size without any outstanding feature that I could detect from the back. They seemed like a couple of black goblins driving silently through the night—and as rough as hell. The small guy looked back and said something in a foreign tongue and the driver grunted but didn't look.

After another half hour we pulled into a small farmhouse that was either red brick or an imitation and, of course, two-storied. They pulled around in the back and under some sort of shed that served as a garage. The big one grabbed me by an arm and muscled me out like I didn't weight a hundred and ninety pounds. He hoisted me up to a shoulder and went inside with me.

The smaller one lit a candle in a front room and I saw that it was furnished temporarily and hadn't been lived in for some time. There were two cots and a box on which was spread a lot of junk, shaving equipment, a foreign make of gun and a few scattered cartridges, a pen knife ...

He dumped me on the floor, my head striking and stunning me quickly enough so I didn't yelp or start. I'd been drugged and intended to stay that way for a while.

I think I slipped back into the void for some time because when I revived again dawn was coming in at the windows, grey and drab in widow's weeds. Outside the rain dripped incessantly but there was no other sound. I noticed that the two cots were empty so they must be sleeping in another part of the house. I tested the cords and discovered that I was no Samson; they would have held a large steer. When finally it was light they came back and with them, yawning, was a thick-bellied Nordic.

"Drugged?" he asked.

"Yes," said the big man in English. Evidently they spoke in English because it was their only mutual tongue.

The big man chuckled. "And what would they say? Luckily they were killed trying. I do not understand it. Rubio dead, Karl dead, Lansa and Dedtt dead, Tardara and Altman dead. None wounded. All dead."

I quit peeking because it was dangerous.

The fat German grunted. "The Americans are getting smart although it vas not smart of dem not to take prisoners. They might have made somevone talk."

The gorilla man chuckled. "And what would they say? At this moment I do not know why we took this man. Karl knew what he was to get but not why. Do you?"

The German grunted again. "Maybe ve find oudt. I vould like to know."

"I know two others who wanted to know," said the smaller man in a soft voice that might have been nurtured in Spain. "They are not with us now."

The German churned out a belly deep chuckle. "Don't vorry, liddle man. Emil Stordt iss no fool. Vhen does dis vun come oudt of it?"

The smaller man said. "The doctor told us what to use. He didn't say how long."

"Und vhere iss diss doctor?"

"The police have him."

"So? Den ve vill need anoder one. Maybeso to give truth serum. Dere vas a mistake vunce. Did dis man attend der conference?"

"We don't know. He could not be followed. He may have."

"Und Norcross und der odders?"

"We didn't have enough men to follow them all. We chose this man because he has not long been an operative."

"Ve vill need a doctor. Albert, you vill stay mit der prisoner. Ramon, you und I vill go get der doctor."

"What doctor?"

"De vorld iss full mitt dem. Ve vill visit der helpful Herr Ransome who suggested der vun now heldt by der police."

"The one who got us the other doc?"

"You iss a smart lad, Ramon. Der same."

As soon as the jeep left I sat up. There was no longer any point in playing dead since Albert had composed himself on a cot and wasn't bothering to watch me. After a while his snores sounded and I began to look for some means to cut my bonds. He opened his eyes a little later and found me rubbing against the sharp brick at the fireplace. He reached for me and for five minutes he beat me with open hand so as not to murder me, I suppose. Methodically and passionlessly he slapped me around, knocking me over and setting me up again until my face felt like a balloon and my eyes were nearly closed.

"Don't do that again," he said calmly and, taking out a sheath knife from some place about his person, he began to pare fingernails that looked as tough and thick as cow hooves. After whittling them into shape he stretched out again and snored spuriously for a while then sat up.

"Smart, huh?" He grinned fatuously.

"In a manner of speaking. What did you do with Dayne?"

"She is safe."

"She was safe with me."

He grinned wickedly. "Her mother might not think so."

"I wonder what your mother thought when she got her first shocked look at you?"

He was impervious. He shrugged. "Mothers always are a little biased, you know. She probably thought I was cute."

"Only a mother could think that," I said.

"Yes, you're probably correct at that. Did they have that proposed conference with you?"

"I'm small potatoes. I went in the conference room and they handed me a brief case to deliver to the archives. That's all I know and all your truth serum won't get anything else."

He nodded agreeably. "I understand it failed the first time."

"That's where a double mistake was made. I'd already been to the conference but since I didn't know anything I couldn't talk."

"That will be unfortunate. Then there will be no point in letting you live to carry tales."

I didn't relish the subject. "What nationality are you?"

"Albert Oerlika at your service."

"That's doesn't help. What country?"

"I'm a citizen of the New World."

"What's new about it?"

"It will be when we have finished."

"I wish I was free. I'd be over there on top of you in two and one-tenth seconds."

He grinned, showing blackened stumps of teeth. "That would be foolhardly. I am a very strong man."

He didn't use superlatives and didn't need any. We stayed mum for a while and during that time I did a little silent cursing because I hadn't realized that my hands could be in front of me instead of in back; I've pulled that little trick many a time just to keep supple. His knife was stuck in the floor between his feet, but either foot could have cracked my skull so that didn't help.

He yawned and stretched with enough power to have broken my back, great mountains of hard muscle leaping into relief beneath the cloth of his dark shirt.

Outside the rain pattered incessantly and the light was grey like the impending gloom of an early twilight. I went into a sort of gloom myself and twisted this way and that, trying to work some circulation into my cramped hands. My feet were all right but my fingers felt like sticks.

I've read about men staying tied up for hours and then by hook or crook they get loose and go into action like they hadn't just gotten free. Stay tied up that long and see if you can lift a butter knife.

"Mr. Albert?"

Albert levitated a good foot off the cot and came down running, mouthing curses that seemed to be directed at whoever had called him from outside. He hadn't gone ten feet when I started rolling and falling. In a second I had knocked the knife over and, grabbing it in my teeth, turtled back to my spot near the fireplace. I tried to drop it behind a crude old straw hearth broom and almost had a fit when it fell outside. I picked up the broom twice with my teeth and dropped it before I could entice it to fall outside the knife. Then I shoved them both back against the wall and sat back a good six feet away in my old position, sweat dripping and my heart beating a tattoo against my ribs. I tried to count the splinters I had picked up but it was a tedious job. Luckily he had dusted me up very well when he slapped me around because the filth would have given the deal away otherwise.

He came back immediately bringing a big tray covered with a clean cloth and a few sheets of newspapers. The newspapers were freckled with raindrops.

"Kid that brings food twice a day," panted Albert, his face still black with rage. "Forgot about him. Glad he didn't try to come in. One corpse to dispose of is plenty."

"Cheerful son of a bitch, ain't you?"

"Quite. I have a great sense of humor."

He put the food down and went back to bring in a big coffee pot that steamed in a manner to remind me of hunger.

Albert regained his temper and made a spread for himself on top of the box. There were succulent sausages done to a mouth-watering brown, several tremendous stacks of wheat cakes, a bottle of red molasses and a big hunk of country butter. I sat and drooled while he ate his and the other two men's portions, drinking enough coffee to take a bath in during the process. He never even offered me a cup of coffee so I just sat there and suffered.

He belched audibly several times and smoked a cigarette. Then stretched out on the cot.

"Watch it," I said, "you'll fall asleep after that big feed and I'll snap my bonds."

He got up with an uneasy frown and inspected them carefully. "They'll hold. But just to make sure you don't rub on that chimney corner. I'll fix that. He took another of the cots and placed it across the fireplace and tied the legs stoutly with the same brand of cord that held me so firmly.

"Get that loose," he said with a grin, "and I'll hear you."

That was no lie because he had secured it to huge wrought iron nails that had been driven into the wood near the fireplace for some obscure reason and any attempt to move them would have made the rickety mantel give tongue.

I yawned and stretched out. "Well, might as well get some shuteye myself."

And damned if I didn't. When I woke up nothing had changed. The day wasn't any lighter or brighter and the rain still seeped down monotonously.

I sat up and saw that Albert was sleeping like a man his size with a bellyful should. I took a deep breath and looked about, planning my action. I needed a club for him and I couldn't see any.

I examined the far cot to see if I could get one of the stretch sticks out of it but gave that up. If you've ever set up one of those things you know why. While I studied it a shape came into being beneath the cheap shoddy blanket. The longer I looked the more it looked like a firearm of some sort and the better I felt. True, I could have knifed Albert in his sleep, but we needed him too badly for that. I was convinced now that I had located a subgun or something and all my strategy depended on it. I inched over toward the fireplace until I reached the broom; then, like a mouse taking the first look after dark, I eased my hands down behind the straw and managed to make my half-dead fingers get the knife. Fifteen minutes later, numb with fatigue, cramps and pure nervous exhaustion, I felt my hands come free. I brought the knife around, not paying much attention to the blood on it from where I had made several miscues, laid it carefully down and massaged life back into my hands. That was a rest from my previous efforts and when I cut my feet free I felt pretty good.

I thought about rolling to avoid any floor creaks but decided against it, although it was a good idea. I didn't know how good until later. With all care I stood up and took several carefully tested steps across the floor without too much noise. Then it happened, one of those things that you can't be prepared for. A long splinter slid into a hole in my shoe sole, a hole I didn't even know was there, and brought me to the floor with a crash that almost bounced Albert on the cot.

Everything happened at once. I leaped to my feet and made a dive for the gun on the cot just as Albert boiled off his cot and came for me. I had lost the knife as I fell and it was well out of reach so I had to get that gun. It was there, all right, but it turned out to be a cheap little tiny thing that they used to give away for selling two dozen cans of goose grease. It used twenty-two short ammunition. I whirled and didn't even try to shoot it; I just did my best to wrap it around Albert's small thick head. It caught him along the jaw and side of the head and I could feel the bones of his jaw crush under the impact but it accomplished two things. The blow that knocked Albert sprawling also split the stock and away went the only part of the weapon that was any good to me—the barrel. I had to have it so I went after it in a long dive and that surprising animal got there only a little after I did. I swung it to his head again and burst away a section of of his scalp that fell down over his ear like a shaggy red patch.

But he still wasn't out. He got up, slower this time, blood dribbling from his mouth and the hideous tear on his head that was gory now where the white skull had been showing through. I must have been hysterical the next time he charged because I misjudged his speed and struck him at the base of his thick neck with my wrists, effectively disarming myself. He had me then, avoided a knee that might have cracked his pelvis, whirled me around and let me have one of the hardest blows I ever blocked in my life. I caught it with my forearm but even so there was enough force behind it to slam my wrist into my nose, making blood spurt and sending me reeling across the room where I sat down heavily—right on top of the knife. I had it before he could get to me and as he came down I sank it right up to the fist in his thick middle. He let loose a hoarse scream and staggered away from me, but as I got up he came right on back again. Albert had enough vitality for a dozen men and proved it when he avoided a second upthrust and got both hands on my windpipe. He squeezed until red aching darts of pain shot through my brain but all that time I was doing my best to rip him to ribbons. I tried the left side, yanked steel out in a wiping motion and then up into the chest area, rammed as deep as both hands could drive it. When it came away that time it was followed by a hot cascade of blood. The last thrust went all the way to the hilt beneath his left armpit and away I fell into a black bottomless well.

When I came to I couldn't move. A great weight was pressing down on me and I was too weak to lift it off until I heard the jeep pull up into the yard. That did it and in a split second I had wriggled from under the slashed bloody mess that had been Albert and darted drunkenly into the other room to look for a weapon. Frantically I searched the coats hung on a rack, a glad-stone that lay open on a rough rickety table. In the glad-stone I found a beautiful new Walther P-38, loaded and ready to go. For the first time in many hours I was myself again. I felt actually lighthearted as I heard them come into the room and heard the German's startled, *"Herr Gott in Himmel!"*

"You might get a chance to meet Him, Fatty," I said, presenting the Walther and me in the proper sequence.

Neither the whey-faced German nor Ramon needed any orders regarding the preferred positions of their hands.

"Thanks, Herr Schidt," I said as blandly as I could through my macerated throat.

"Vhat for?" he quavered.

"For reminding me that we have been too deadly with weapons. You and Ramon will go back as my prisoners."

Ramon had been easing behind the fat man and took that moment to break for the door. I waited until he was neatly framed in the aperture and loosed a single round which caught him between the shoulder blades and pitched him face first out into the yard.

"You next, *schweinhund?*" I suggested, hefting the Walther suggestively.

"Nein," he quavered. He rattled off some *hoch Deutsch* that I hadn't read in any spy stories.

"Speak English," I ordered. I don't *spraeken sie* much damn *Deutsch."*

He quivered like a mountain of jelly and went grayer than ever.

"Achtung!" I roared suddenly and had the mean satisfaction of seeing him snap to ramrod attention that gradually wilted as he realized he had been bitten. "So, one of Hitler's own. That's nice to know. Now, abouten the facen and marche. *Deutschland Uber Alles.* Pig fertilizer!"

He turned, went out and stepped shudderingly over the still figure of Ramon in the yard where a widening red stain had begun to show in the rainwater.

"You drive and I'll sit in the back and this marvelous weapon shall be aimed steadily at your pelvis. A man remains a painful paralytic wreck for the rest of his life if he's shot there. You will neither speak nor will you look around until you reach Pennsylvania Avenue, at an address which I shall delight in pointing out."

He was a thoroughly beaten man and followed orders which was fine with me because I stayed in a partial coma and roused only when we made DuPont Circle. I gave further orders and in twenty minutes I was talking with Norcross, Soldarez and the chief.

CHAPTER SIX

"THEY USED THE fire escape," the chief was saying, "and they had already arrived before Waynne and Polaski took their positions. It was done so smoothly and swiftly that Morrison didn't have time to make his rounds. They'd probably have gotten him, too."

"How did they get the others?" I asked because I liked Polaski a lot.

"Sapped them and tied them up. They were there all ready and waiting for Morrison to cut them loose. By that time there was no sign of the thugs or you."

"What about Dayne?" I had been afraid to ask but I had to know.

There was a silence which Soldarez broke. "There hasn't been a trace of her, Ches."

I felt like dying. "Think you'll get anything out of that fat boy I brought in?"

"We can try," said the chief. "What happened to the others? You look like you've been swimming in a blood pit."

"One named Albert Oerlika—that's where all the blood came from—and a little fellow named Ramon something. At a little abandoned farm house out beyond Bethesda about fifteen miles. We went right by the National Naval Medical Center."

I sort of lost interest in the talk and when I returned to relative awareness I was speeding toward my place with Phil driving my car.

We went up the stairs with me barely making it and when I fell out on the couch a red-eyed Lonzo came foaming out of the kitchen to arm me up and kiss me resoundingly on both cheeks.

I managed to get him off and make motions that I was starved. That made all the difference and he ducked back into the kitchen and began to send forth mouthwatering smells.

"I'm afraid we're through here," said Soldarez. "You should get a load of chow aboard and sleep. When you wake, Alonzo and I will have packed everything and all we'll have to do is board a plane. Where do you store your car?"

"That car's fiction. It belongs to Frank Barber. He has two and lets me use one. I might as well tell you, Phil—I'm not going a step until I hear something from Dayne."

He didn't say anything. Then a certain electric tension seeped through the fog in my brain. I looked around, not to see a man, but a figure with a face carved like a mask.

It was as devoid of pleasantness as a gargoyle and as hard as deck teak. His eyes were blobs of black obsidian with a tiny spot of molten fire in each. His lips moved and his words sounded like the hiss of a bush master. "They could have been wrong about you, I suppose."

He got up and disappeared into the second bedroom and didn't come out until I had finished eating, although the savor was gone and I felt like a punished school kid.

"All right," I said after a while. "So the world is more important than Dayne and me. My feelings don't count for anything. I'm not even supposed to have any."

Phil smiled frostily. "I haven't said a word."

"You produced the most dramatic silence of any man I have ever met."

"I accept the compliment. Had you really thought things out when you said that? Are you forgetting that you were drugged? Or did you drug yourself?"

I hadn't thought of that angle and I don't know why because it was certainly the thing I should have thought of. I slumped in my chair so weak and mentally beaten that I couldn't even think. I was conscious only of a great void of bitter pain inside me. "Where are we going?"

"We're going to Merida, Yucatan. I've already taken the liberty of reserving rooms at the Hotel Merida."

"What's the idea? And put up at the biggest joint there—which the Merida is, if I remember my travel folders?"

"Several reasons. We want to be noticed, for one thing. Norcross is leaving tomorrow for South Africa and environs."

"That I can see. There were some robberies there but your robberies occurred on the high seas."

Phil massaged his hard face thoughtfully. "Think back when we were listening to Rubio give his last words. What were they?"

"Something about Sierra and a lot of mumbling."

"You didn't maybe get the word 'Nero?' "

"Umm…maybe. Not too good, though. He mouthed a lot of things."

"I thought at the time he had said something about Sierra Nero, which is a mumble might have been intended to be 'Negro'."

"Washington's full of them."

"Of Afro-Americans, yes, but so far as I know there is no Sierra Negro around here."

"Black mountain, huh? Do you have one spotted?"

Phil massaged his slim muscular hands. "We're all shooting in the dark, Ches. I know where there is a Sierra Negro and I doubt that they could find a better hideout. Maybe I'm all wet and the chances are great that I am. But since Sierra Negro is in our territory then it's up to us to find out."

I felt a little tingle of excitement. "What exactly is Sierra Negro?"

"It's a volcanic island. Draw a line from the Yucatan Peninsula to Cuba, then finish the triangle about twenty degrees south of

Habana and Merida. That's Sierra Negro. There are all sorts of legends about the place. Pirate treasure is supposed to be buried there. People used to go there as a lark to hunt for buried treasure and that sort of thing, but some strange things happened to the last few parties and now no one goes there. Sort of a twentieth century haunt on the place."

While I wandered around in a three-quarters fog, Phil and Lonzo did the needful things. All I could do was see the patrician elegance of Dayne's walk, the smooth purity of her skin and the glaze of her eyes when rocked by a passion that neither of us had ever tasted before.

We ate lunch—at any rate, I'm told we did—and the next thing I knew we were on a Constellation; the Washington Monument was drifting past the wing tip and fading into the background of blue distance. I sat in something of a trance for a while and though it didn't seem like several hours I knew it must be when the irregular shore of Lake Ponchartrain showed below us and the wing flaps began to groan outward. After a wait of twenty minutes we were airborne again and beneath us was nothing but a stretch of unending blue, Gulf of Mexico blue, decorated tastefully with pristine whitecaps and an occasional skimming sea bird. After a little more than two hours the pure white beaches of Yucatan beckoned near the horizon and the water that had taken on a greenish cast was now dotted with small sailboats like toy vessels in a gigantic bathtub. Again the landing flaps were rolled out protestingly and we swung around into the wind, gliding over huge henequin plantations spotted here and there with brown patches of com. We landed and coasted up to the apron where we could see numerous smiling brown people watching the arrival. We went through a door marked *Inspecciones* and answered some questions asked in bad English until Phil spoke a few reams of breathless Spanish; then things changed like magic. In a second we were in the customs office where a fat Yucatecan bowed and waved a grand hand at baggage inspection. Before I knew what was going on we were being piled into a yellow Nash, vintage prewar but still able to chuff along under the guidance of someone whose name was Pepe.

We rattled away from the airport and headed for Merida which glowed whitely in the distance. We rode past the slaughter house with its population of *sopilotes,* which moved the driver to say something in Spanish and laugh.

"He says," interpreted Phil, "that the *sopilotes,* buzzards, are Merida's flying sanitation department. Not a bad analogy."

"I can't think of a buzzard as being very sanitary," I said.

"Possibly not the most sanitary of birds but what they remove so expeditiously would be a great deal less so. They're worth their weight in spoiled meat in the tropics."

The *Parque Centenario* we passed next with laughing children playing under the trees and looking at monkeys and strange exotic birds in cages, which moved the driver to spout more Spanish.

"He says," put in Lonzo, not wanting to be outdone as interpreter, "that they have an African lion but no jaguars in the park. The jaguar figures in the ancient Mayan religion."

Well, it was all very interesting but between Dayne and the dinner I'd passed up on the plane I was torn in both heart and stomach. The sun was setting in a mass of crimsons, blues, golds and all shades in between but though I remember giving it momentary attention it didn't make much of an impression on me.

Down *Calle Secenta* we went past the *Plaza Grande* with its vendors of fruit, sweetmeats and a lot of things I couldn't identify; then the tremendous cathedral that looked as old as time itself, past pink stuccoed buildings with walls two feet thick to a smaller plaza and church and then a gigantic theater. Finally we saw the lofty white walls of the Hotel Merida that soared majestically above the lower buildings around it. We were swarmed under by jacketed bellhops, saluted by the cop who must stand at the door all day and half the night. Fernando Barbachano Junior came to greet us. He and Phil wrung each other's hands until I wondered if they had known each other; when they embraced and smote each other on the back, I knew they had. The Barbachanos, Junior and Senior, go together like rum and lime. They're the sort of people who believe in the personal touch and every time you look around they are chatting entertainingly with guests or offering to buy drinks, an offer which is more often accepted than refused.

After introductions and signing the register we were hustled across a big lobby with slick tiled floors into the elevator and lofted to the seventh floor and a room that might comfortably have housed a family.

I sat on a soft bed and tried to collect myself. I couldn't, so I got up and walked to the window and looked down. There, enclosed in a patio with palms and other exotic plants, was a gem of a swimming pool and in the pool was a gem of a woman. She was tanned creamily and her hair was the color of cordovan leather. She lolled about in the water exhibiting the nerve-rattling shapeliness of her long legs, the firmness of the pouting breasts that seemed about to leap from their frail confinement and the roundness of her arms as they moved lazily through the water. She twisted and went under like a graceful fish, the water turning her body to a startling whiteness. She came up and tossed her hair, then clambered out where an anxious young man leaped for her and enveloped her in a big bath towel. He did it very tenderly, too, but she seemed a little impatient with him and sat down, towel and all, before he could dry her—which seemed to have been his intention.

Phil came from the bathroom suave and fresh, dressed in a worsted uniform that made him look like a modern version of Zorro, ready to ride ghostily through the countryside stab-bing evildoers in the brisket with a rapier. His moustache was micrometically correct, his hair lacquered in place and the piratical fit of his cream-colored uniform made him look a little unbelievable.

"Should I be flattered by your attention?"

"Do, by all means. Don't you feel uncomfortable?"

"Oh, no. I feel like a million and I'm hungry. You look a little all gone."

"I am, but I'm hungry, too, and I find that I can still react to a figure. There's a girl in the pool."

He went to look and I followed to look over his shoulder. She was drying herself now, sitting on the end of the diving board while her lad hovered anxiously at the edge of the pool. One of Phil's eyebrows shot upward and his breath hissed inwardly. "A very tasty morsel, I'd say. Who's the jittery swain?"

"I haven't been introduced to either," I snapped. "And I'm still hungry."

"Wash your face and let's eat."

I went to wash my face and found Lonzo washing his so I had to wait. We went down to the dining room that nestles on the left of the main patio just as you come into the hotel. We took seats in highbacked chairs done in leather with huge brass studs and were waited on by Mayan women in their white embroidered *huipils,* their hair drawn back and seasoned with a big colorful ribbon bow.

One padded up and waited while I looked over the menu that was mouth-watering. Quail, wild duck, venison, roast or chops, steaks, chicken, and half a dozen kinds of fish.

"Order for me," I said wearily. "Make it plenty and make it red meat. Tell 'em to double the potatoes and bread and butter. I'll take a beer now and iced tea with the dinner."

He ordered in Spanish and we started sipping the excellent native Pilsner.

The dinner came faster than I ever saw food come from a kitchen but I didn't argue with the phenomenon. I was too interested in the two thick chops that adorned my plate with piles of brown potatoes. On the side was a dish of fried black beans with a tortilla stuck in the midst of it and it was good, too.

"What sort of meat is this?" I asked.

"Venison," said Lonzo. "You can get all sorts wild game here in the markets."

I ate with a will and soon had it cleared away. Then they brought ice cream and thick strawberry layer cake and strong black coffee. By the time it was all gone I was ready to call it quits.

Phil called a waitress, *"Señorita, deme un paquete de cigarros, Ambajadores, y fósforos, por favor."*

She brought a package of cigarettes and a small box of matches. "Ah," he said sniffing the cigarettes. "At last some real cigarettes. That makes two things we have better than you, Ches. Beer and cigarettes."

What could I do but smile?

After dinner Phil scurried out and left Lonzo and me to our own business, which was to sit around and watch people come and go through the high domed lobby. It was cool and restful sitting in the rattan chairs watching toothsome pulchritude drift in and out. No one was in a hurry and everyone had a kind word for everyone else. Then my girl of the swimming pool came in.

Without her bathing suit and in a dress she still looked good enough for eye-banging. Her shadow was hard on her heels and she didn't look a bit more disposed to honor his presence than she had at the pool. Her face was petulantly cast with deep slumbrous brown eyes, short fluffy brown hair and a skin that made me almost drool. She wore no make-up except a dash of expertly applied lipstick and didn't need any more. Her stride was free and lithe with the same natural grace that had characterized her swimming. She swept a glance toward me that was sizzling but it kept sweeping until it was past me. She turned to the kid and spoke in a low voice, smoothing the cream-colored shantung dress she wore at the waist and hips. It was already fitting in a manner that made Lonzo draw in a hissing breath. The lad didn't seem to relish the idea of what she proposed and pouted about it but obeyed. He went out the door of the hotel and she swung her hot disturbing eyes back to me and considered me for a moment. I looked back because I could see she was doing some fast thinking and I was wondering what it was about. She passed long slim fingers over the provocative bulge of her hips again and started for where we sat. As she approached I stood up and bowed.

"If I stared I hope I'm forgiven," she said in a voice that was like warm honey.

"You were forgiven before that," I said gallantly. "One could not help forgiving you, having once seen you—especially in the pool."

Her smile made a chill run up my back. "Thank you. I'm Verna Martell."

I took her soft warm hand and squeezed it gently. "I'm Chester Markham. Would that your pleasure could equal half of mine."

She smiled, showing off her white regular teeth. "Maybe it can. After all, we've just met."

I remembered Lonzo with a start but when I turned to introduce him he had disappeared. I turned back to her. "I find it a bit difficult to reconcile the unspoken promise of further acquaintance, and possibly a little association, with the lad you apparently sent on an errand."

She arched a slim eyebrow at me. "You saw how obediently he went, didn't you?"

"I did and I marveled at it. I'd prove a lot harder to order."

"Not Jonathan. He is the very soul of propriety and sobriety and conventionality."

I made a face. "You make Jonathan sound rather dull."

"You have no idea how dull."

"Married to him?"

"Heavens, no. I made up my mind to come down here because I love the ruins and Jonathan helped because he's been here before. I ran into opposition from my family and his. They were so trusting of Jonathan, however, they both consented to the trip only if he could accompany me. You see, we were engaged."

"You're not now?"

She shrugged. "I don't know how to explain it. He's a bore and always has been, but he is attentive and I think I was weary of being shoved around here and there, having so-called eligible men thrust at me. To stop it I let myself be ringed by Jonathan and that halted the others. He was gone most of the time on some obscure business and didn't bother me." Her lips curled with disdain. "Shows you what my suitors were like. To some men this emerald would be a challenge. To them it was a sign saying 'Keep Off.' They did."

I thought of an off-color crack then but I didn't say it. Instead I said, "It'll be more comfortable in the bar. I understand drinks are served there."

Her eyes lighted. "Now you're making sense. Personally, I was beginning to wonder if there were any liquor in Yucatan. Jonathan would curl up and die at the thought of me entering a bar."

"Let him," I said leading the way. The bar was dimly lit, with heavy dark wood tables and the ubiquitous high-backed chairs. A waiter, either feeling his oats or his grain, almost danced over to our table and bowed low. "Chino at your service. I shall take your order, deliver it to the bartender verbatim, close my eyes and hope for the best. He rarely disappoints a customer although he often disappoints me. I was in the United States Marine Corps during the war and I speak passable if not flawless English. Will you order?"

Taking a breath after that oration I ordered bourbon and water, and Verna desired a rum and Coke.

He quirked an eyebrow at me and grinned toothily. "Not intending to launch into any heated sort of argument, you'll save money if you drink our Yucatecan brandy. It is quite good, believe me."

"I'll give it a go," I said. "Just trot it out and watch our table carefully."

"I shall and will," he said and with another short choppy bow he spun around and gave our order.

We sipped our drinks and the brandy was good—and cheap. I began to study the way Verna played with her glass, her long fingers rarely still, the rounded perfection of her arms, the creamy tan column of her neck and the lush warm proportions of her face. Her dress was modestly cut at the neck but no cut could restrain the revolutionary upsurge of her breasts. I mentally priced her bra which must have been quite expensive and frail because the points still managed to poke excitingly at the fabric of her dress. When she would shift her position in the chair I thought I could hear the expensive hiss of fragile silken underthings and it seemed I could catch the faint but unequaled fragrance of her clean body, a warm human odor that has no equal.

We chatted in lively fashion about nothing much until the fourth drink; then her eyes began to sparkle and it seemed that her breath came a little faster and her breasts seemed sharper. Her laughter became more unrestrained and she leaned closer to me when she spoke.

I began to wonder if Merida didn't have better facilities for conversation when who should breeze into the bar, his clean-cut face aflame and crew cut on end, but Jonathan.

He marched stiffly to the table and stood even stiffer while he looked down her, his lips trembling with rage. She looked indolently at him and waited.

"This shall be reported back home," he said valiantly restraining his temper.

"How jolly," she said and drained her glass.

"Shameless, that's what you are. Drinking liquor in a bar with a stranger, a—"

"Have a care, sonny," I warned. "We were having fun until you came. Why don't you go buy yourself a bag of sweetmeats and take them to bed with you."

"Sir," he said freezingly, "I was not addressing you. Verna, you will come with me this instant."

"On the contrary, I shall do no such thing. I'm having fun for the first time since I visited Uxmal. Follow the gentleman's suggestion and go to bed with a bag of candy."

"You refuse to leave this place," he shrilled, appalled at the new resistant Verna.

"That is the general idea. I'll see you at breakfast."

He bit his lips for a moment then turned and stalked away.

"I think Johnny's respectably put out," I said, downing the last of my *habeñero*.

"So it would seem. Ches, let's go on the town."

"That's the best idea since you decided to chuck Johnny. Chino."

"Yes, señor."

"We want a place to go and dance. Can you recommend one?"

"I can, señor. I suggest the Tulipanes. There is a *cenote* there—an underground pool. You may swim, dance, dine or just sit and make poems to the moon."

"Sounds like fairyland. But why would I make poems to the moon with a lady like this present?"

"Señor, pardon the familiarity, but North Americans are a little crazy. Witness the lady's erstwhile escort."

"You have me there. We're not all like him. By the way, where can we get a cab?"

"One block down at the Plaza. Or I can have one come to the hotel entrance."

"We'll walk," I said and we did, slowly and without any apparent destination. We passed a smartly uniformed policemen who smiled, touched his cap and murmured, *"Buenos noches"* in soft Spanish.

Oddly there wasn't a single taxi available at the moment, so we walked past the statue to motherhood in the center of the small plaza to where several of the little carriages awaited in rank, shining with shoe polish and ready to jog us to any place in town for a pittance.

We made a signal to the *cochero* and I said, in questionable Spanish, *"¿ Sabe usted Tulipanes?"*

He nodded and tapped the halfpint horse with a switch and we began our short-lived journey.

CHAPTER SEVEN

WE WHIPPED AROUND the square and passed the police-man again, who apparently hadn't moved from the spot where he stood tapping himself on the lower leg with a heavy stick of *zapote* wood. We had drawn slightly past him when a yell and sudden activity behind us made the *cochero* pull his little nag to a sliding halt, throwing us against what would be the dash-board in a more modern conveyance.

Instantly it seemed the street was filled with chattering peo-ple. We got out and saw the policeman standing over a prone figure, the stick still held tightly in his hand, the hand that had evidently just used it. From the distance he had covered he must have sprung like a jaguar and it is certain that he had lowered the boom on the bird in such a manner as to make him a messy sight indeed. The back of his head was mush and his eyes looked like they were popped almost from his head. From his nose ran a trickle of bloody fluid. More interesting still was the long-bar-reled Mauser that lay some six feet from his fingers that were now gradually drawing up like the legs of a dying fly.

People milled about talking a steady stream, the policeman blew shrill repeated blasts on his whistle and bedlam grew by leaps and bounds. Green-clad soldiers arrived from down *Calle Secenta* with rifles and fixed bayonets and other policemen arrived from every direction and pretty soon you couldn't hear yourself think. Then right in the midst of it all Soldarez stepped out of a taxi, dazzling in uniform, and let go a clarion shout that had all eyes on him in a second and in another second the noise died like magic. He gave rapid orders in Spanish, the soldiers saluted and began to clear the civilians out of the area and the policemen busied themselves talking to their colleagues and searching the area for more like the one on the sidewalk.

Finally I got in the big question. "Phil, what the hell's this all about?"

He looked at me and grinned, giving Verna a short choppy bow. "We have been noticed," he said. "The policeman just about split this guy's skull with his stick in time to prevent a murder."

"Whose murder?" I asked.

"Yours." He turned and started talking to the policeman again, leaving me to the peculiar comfort of knowing my life had just been saved.

When it had been all whipped out, this was what had happened. The man had evidently followed us and had taken his own good time in choosing his spot. The spot had been a wide dark doorway which, when I took stock, showed that the policeman had after all moved nearly half a block. He had not advertised the move so that when the man emerged from the doorway and leveled his gun the law didn't stop to ask silly questions—he just bounded to the attack and dealt the intended assassin a shattering blow with the heavy stick. The one blow had been sufficient.

A growling police car pulled up and disgorged a personage whose attire spoke of rank. He began to give the policeman merry hell until he saw Soldarez. Then things changed abruptly.

There were more hugs and back slaps. Then I noticed my savior was sweating from the blasting he had taken so I stepped up and told Phil, "Tell his honor that this man acted with deadly dispatch and unerring judgment. To him I owe the fact that I'm alive. I congratulate him on the quality and resourcefulness of his men. I consider his force a credit to the whole of Mexico."

Phil must have made it as good or better than I spoke it because the chief beamed proudly and shook my hand. Then he patted the beat man on the back and all was forgiven.

Verna through it all had stood placidly beside me and hadn't uttered a word. There was a warm spot on my arm where she had been leaning slightly but there was none of the screaming woman about her.

"Now do you think we can proceed to a night of revelry?" she asked.

"Aren't you afraid to go about with a marked man?"

Her eyes sparkled. "I haven't had so much fun in all my life. You're my sort of man. What are you, by the way?"

"All is a great secret," I whispered. My designation is Operative XK-4."

"You're kidding but it wouldn't surprise me. Are you and that lovely man in the uniform together?"

"In a manner of speaking."

"Then I know it's true. He's the type."

"I wear better," I said.

"No doubt. He's lovely but not my sort. I prefer them more like you."

Phil came over and was introduced. "Where were you going?" he asked.

I think I blushed. "Well, I didn't expect anything to happen tonight so I thought Verna and I would take in a club. I guess that's out."

He massaged his chin. "It should be, but I do hate to interrupt your fun." He turned about and searched the fringes of a crowd until he saw whom he wanted and beckoned. From the crowd came a small squarely-built Mexican, swarthy, with a wide expressionless face. He wore a white *guayabera* and coarse white trousers. In Merida there were thousands like him. Phil spoke to him rapidly, then turned to us. "Have fun. It's all right now. Pepe'll look after you."

I put Verna back into the *coche* and turned to Phil. "What's up?"

He inclined his head toward the girl. "Is she clean?"

"She bathes regularly," I said stiffly.

"Ass! Who, what is she?"

"I don't know. She's the girl in the pool. I'd say she's okay."

"All right. You're supposed to have some intelligence. Just watch your step. Got your gun?"

I patted the lump under my white coat. "Yeah."

"Good. Don't be afraid to use it. We have *carte blanche* here. I've explained to Colonel Montejo as much as I can. He has assured us of every cooperation."

I grunted. "We got cooperation before we asked for it. Who's that little man you spoke to?"

"One of the best shots in Mexico and he knows how to blend with the scenery. He never sleeps and he's reliable to the last degree."

"That's good. I feel better now."

I felt better still a few minutes later. Verna stretched her legs out and writhed like a snake, her body filling the dress until I was afraid it would burst a seam, especially where the breasts fought at the front. She relaxed and let her dreamy eyes drift over to me. "What are you thinking, Ches?"

"I'm thinking that you should be locked up—or I should. It isn't safe for us to be together under this moon the way you are under that dress."

Her smile was slow. "You don't know how I am under this dress."

"It doesn't leave much to the imagination and I saw you in the pool, remember?"

"In that case I'm going to say something very unladylike."

"Good. What?"

"Quit chipping your teeth and kiss me."

The conveyance was sort of bumpy and I missed my goal the first two times but I made it the third time and it seemed like I had fallen into a vacuum. My ears roared as my blood pressure went sky high. Her lips were petal soft, parted, warm and eager and her body supported their actions to the last degree. Her back was strong with a deep muscular trench that I explored inch by inch until, feeling that I might, I covered one taut throbbing breast with my hand. She stiffened and a little throaty whine rose only to be muffled by the contact of our lips. She tore away and gasped deeply as the demands of her breathing became more than her nose could provide.

She clutched me hard and buried her face in the curve of my neck, sending torrents of heated air down my open collar which made me nearly faint with the novel sensation.

"Oh, Ches! What you *do* to me!"

"What?"

"You shouldn't ask. I can't tell you."

"Is it intimate?"

"Very. What a sheltered life I must have lived, else I wouldn't be a virgin. There aren't men like you where I come from."

"You haven't met them. They're there."

"Maybe. Anyhow I've met you. That's my number one concern. Do you think we could stand another kiss like the last one?"

I grinned. "It won't be like the last one. Fair warning."

It wasn't like the last one because I twisted my mouth hard against hers until I could taste the tip of her hesitant tongue and drew her in until she was bent in a fabulous semicircle. My fingers manipulated the neck of her dress until it was open to the waist and then I shifted my attention to her throat and the early rises of her breasts where the pressure of her spidery brassiere cut into the soft flesh, the strained position having thrust them into greater prominence. She moaned through clenched teeth and her hands locked themselves in back of my head, forcing me so close against her that my face was buried in the sweet flesh and my breath cut off. The sensation was so novel that I let her hold me until the blood was pounding at my temples and I had to make her release me to avoid suffocation.

"What do you think?" I asked, smoothing her disordered hair back from her forehead.

She gasped for breath a few times and shook her head. "If they get better that fast maybe we'd better stop. I don't think I can stand much more. Tell me what I should do, Ches. Please, tell me."

"Nope, I won't do that. If you have any qualms you'd better let me take you back to the hotel."

"And Jonathan?"

"And Jonathan."

She shuddered but her head came up and her eyes were very level and steady. "Thanks, no. I'll go with you."

"Do you know what it could mean?"

"At the moment that's what I want it to mean. I'm dying by inches, Ches. Let's don't go to Tulipanes."

"Your eagerness is flattering. But there are other things to consider. This will be your first time, won't it?"

"Actually, yes, but only technically. I'm healthy and normal and I know I have a lovely body. I'm aware of it. I also know that there are heights of joy it should bring me, unbelievable and shattering to experience. I have sinned many times but only mentally. Now I want to sin in fact. I want it to be a glorious sin that is like a white hot fire to blast loose all the conflict and dammed up … everything in me. No wonder women reared as I have been never know what it is. They can't."

I felt a little odd, listening to a lovely girl plan her first seduction with a gleam in her eye and logic and objectivity in her mind.

"As long as you know what you're about and can feel that way about it, all right. However, there's no rush. It's not good to rush and don't fall in love with me."

"Why not?"

I told her about Dayne without giving anything away about my objective. She nodded her head and looked out into the moon-splashed darkness. I could see a suspicion of moisture at the corners of her eyes.

"I can see what you mean." She turned back to me. "Why did she leave you like that?"

"I don't think she had any choice." I didn't think any such thing. That was why it hurt to think about her. I couldn't forget that she had been the only one who could have doped the drinks.

"You mean she was taken away?"

"Something like that."

"And that's why you're down here?"

"Partly."

"Ches, if you love her how can you make such beautiful love to me?"

"Because a man's not like a woman. I've got an awful lot of love in me. That probably doesn't make sense to you."

She pondered for a while. "On the contrary, it does. I had to tear my mind out of the conventional way of thinking for a moment. It was an effort but I made it. I think I know what you mean. If I can provide love why shouldn't you take it?"

"You're getting warm. Actually, I may never see her again. Grief involves too much personal pride to indulge in it like taking medicine."

She sighed and leaned over with her back to me. She caught my wrists and brought them around front to place them over her breasts: then she quietly began to have small rapturous convulsions until at last she shoved hard backward against me, held it for a moment, then collapsed and began to weep.

"I'm sorry to cry," she said after a time, "but it was such a relief. I just couldn't wait."

I kissed her on the neck and nodded. "I know how it is and I think you were a little conservative when you said you were normal. You're super-normal."

She twisted her neck and kissed me sweetly, clingingly but without passion. I returned it but I couldn't keep it on such a level nor could she when the impact struck her.

We arrived at the big wall surrounding Tulipanes and she had to hurry up the buttoning processes, comb her hair and touch up her lips.

They seated us in the open, facing a bandstand on which were several native musicians who were strictly in a class by themselves. We sat there with untouched drinks at our elbows until they had finished the song then we relaxed.

"Ches, did you ever hear anything so beautiful?"

"Not that I remember." I swigged down half a gill of *habeñero* and felt the renewed burn creep eagerly through my stomach. I felt other-worldish like I was in another sphere and their next song, a dreamy tango called *Santa,* made me feel even more so.

I had at one time been able to cut a mean tango so I led Verna to the floor and proceeded to prove I could still do it.

We wove in and out of its smooth figures with her following like a trained veteran, as supple as a reed, light on her feet and completely in tempo with the music. Her breath came faster and her eyes made the stars look actually dowdy. Her body twisted smoothly as she danced with utter released flexibility that cannot ever be achieved by someone never touched by passion; most dances were dances of passion in their early days and to dance them properly still demands something of that nature. One only needs see a Cuban couple do a real rhumba and he will realize that our watered-down version, which is really a *son,* can't touch the McCoy.

Santa came to its whispered ending and the band went into a beguine that was modestly paced with a deep blood stirring rhythm in which chattering *moracas,* the stacatto *claves* and finger drums played the major roles. White lights were replaced by red ones and Verna underwent a transformation also. From the relatively staid but uninhibited tango she went right into a rhumba that made sweat start out on my face. There was nothing blatantly wanton or lewd about it. When that occurs all you have is exhibitionism for its own sake. She was simply a body that seemed without bones, all rhythm, all sinuous motion, a devotee to nature's strongest call; the way she performed it, if she were wrong then the whole scheme of all fundamental things is wrong.

Others stopped and watched us, even those who were really better-versed in the fine points of the dance than we. They watched because there was something contagious about the way she threw herself into the spirit of the music and they knew that they were seeing something rare. At the end she almost collapsed against me and I led her trembling back to the table amid astounded honest applause from our audience.

A waiter appeared mopping his face. "Allow me to present the admiration of the entire house, *señor* and *señorita*. It was superb, a masterful dance. Will you accept drinks on your hosts?"

I nodded happily. "We'll be glad to." And in a few seconds they were there.

She sipped her drink and reached over to touch my hand, her eyes looking unnaturally large in the half light. "It happened again," she said breathlessly. "Ches, what a marvelous man you are."

"Don't lay it all on me," I said swallowing a sufficiency of *habeñero*. "It's you, largely."

She nodded rapidly. "I guess so. It's me wanting out so badly that I synthesize it with just a little stimulation."

I grinned. "You can blame the last on me if you wish."

The hand returned to mine and the eyes were honest and steady. "I love it here, Ches, but I want to leave now."

I frowned and got up from the table, beckoning to the waiter. I met him and drew him into the shadows of a thatched hut. "Where can a man take a señorita where it will be quiet and he won't be disturbed?"

The waiter bit his lips and nodded slowly. "I do not know of a place, señor, that I could recommend wholeheartedly. However, there is a small park..." He shrugged dramatically. "Unless you demand superior appointments there are always the shrubs and the grass. Some little thatched huts where picnic people get out of the sun." He grinned. "Only at night there are no picnic people."

We rode slowly through the night with the pony taking his time and the moon making a goddess of Verna. She lay across me, her head in the crook of my arm where she could reach my lips at will. Her left breast was a golden white mound with steep rounded sides, tipped with the most succulent shade of deep pink where the moon caressed it softly. Her left leg was nearly bare; a breeze had lifted her dress and she hadn't bothered to pull it down. I kissed her and let the full flickering surcharge of passion creep into it, wrenching a groan from her depths. My hand found the naked leg and the touch was like a ravening shock to my supersensitive hand.

Her body gave a great leap and I was forced to hold her tightly, stopping for a moment an intended foray into forbidden territory. The hand went back and although she stiffened again I didn't have to remove it to hold her. Slowly it crept up, tasting every inch of marble smooth surface that was soft and slightly damp and warm with an ineffable sweetness that made of my hand a creature of all five senses. She withdrew her mouth from mine to gasp out incoherent pleas and lave my neck and face with her lips in a frantic excess of tumultuous response.

"Ches... Ches..." Her teeth sank into my shoulder but the pain was a pleasure and shortly thereafter I discovered how strong she was; I needed both hands to hold her in the vehicle. She collapsed after a short while, sobbing and clutching my sides painfully.

For a few moments she was quiet; then she lifted her dewy face and looked at me, her lips trembling slightly, petal-soft and burnished from her recent endeavors. "Ches, she doesn't love you like I do."

"How do you know?"

"She can't. I know that." She sat up. "And I'll show you. I know I can. Even though this will be something entirely new to me, yet it isn't new. That sounds silly, I know, but it's the way I feel. Make me a promise, Ches. If I can make myself a force, let me in, will you? Let me make of the moment what I can and don't throw up a wall against me. Promise?"

I nodded, feeling a thick ache in my throat. "I promise." Somehow I was beginning to feel that this would be one promise that I might not have a lot of trouble keeping.

The *coche* stopped and without turning his head the driver said, *"Este es el parque, señor."*

I stepped out and helped her down, then spent a few minutes making the driver understand that he should wait for us. He nodded, smiling inscrutably, and began to fashion a rough cigarette.

We walked through narrow crushed stone passages between flowers, orange, grapefruit and lemon trees. Coconut palms, royal palms and feathery poincianas and tamarinds formed the main sentinels while the sharp heavy scent of frangipani loaded the cool air with a fragrance that was almost palpable. Bushes of scarlet hibiscus showed darkly along the borders of the walk that gradually led us into a natural *cul-de-sac* at one end of which was an arbor covered thickly with bougainvillea.

Verna sighed and came very close to me. I pressed her closer and allowed her to flow into every outline of my body. She looked up. "This is a private little corner of heaven, Ches. It's ours for now. Listen to the quiet. No one within miles." I listened and heard the subdued hum of the city in the distance. It seemed very far away. I kissed her and surpassed all previous efforts, releasing her finally because she whimpered like a hurt child. But I could see from the greenish depths of her eyes that it was only the mightiest force of nature driven past endurance.

Suddenly her dress fell at her feet, leaving only the whispering silk of a half slip and the loosened bra to cover her. She let me look, shivering and biting her lower lip.

"I can feel your eyes, Ches, like hot fingers touching me."

"No man on earth could erect a wall against you unless he had been caponized."

She smiled and gently lifted the bra and let it fall on top of the dress. Unconsciously she drew in her stomach and arched her back until her breasts were exultantly lifted like pyramids of the finest materials glistening smoothly in the cool white moonlight, peaked sharply and palpitant with repressed urgency. I caught her to me and dallied until she was weeping and gripping me painfully. She struggled free and stood back again, hooking her thumbs into the elastic waist of the half slip and skidding it downward until it could grip nothing and fell at her feet.

The pale blue briefs followed it and she stood straight and unashamed in the moonlight, a picture of stupefying joy, a monument to all that was finest and richest in womanhood.

I caught her to me in a fever, driving her breath from her body with the ferocity of my grip. She weakened and almost fainted in my arms and I knew that again her bounding nature had sent her into the thin upper air of madness unable to withstand the forces that pounded at her door. I picked her up and went to the little arbor and found that inside was a broad wooden bench over which someone had draped a clean mat. I placed her across it and she fell limply into a shape of sublime grace, like a vestal virgin across the altar of sacrifice. Splotched with filtered moonlight, she reminded me of some unearthly spotted cat in repose with steel hard muscles mistily suggestive through skin of surpassing softness.

In a moment I was back and her breath went out in a long soft sigh that seemed to rattle in her throat. She was hot and moist and so soft to the touch that my throat contracted achingly.

"Please, Ches…" Her head went slowly back, her bottom lip caught hard between her teeth. She tensed as sensation leaped through her veins and nerves, her eyes widened and her arms clutched me hard. "Gently, Ches…" A little song rose in her throat. "Gently… Don't hurt me… too much…"

I did not hurt her too much and Verna made good her promise to be something to me no one else had ever been before. I was rather like a chilled observer watching divinity descend from the heavens on a stairway of gold made glittering by moonbeams and overlorded by the heavy blanket of frangipani. The night had grown so old that it was young again, looking toward the new day, when at last we walked down the graveled path to where the *cochero* lay asleep in his conveyance.

We woke him and bade him take it slow as we were still loathe to part, especially after the closeness of the hours just past.

"I knew it," she whispered. "I think I knew it when I first saw you in the lobby. It came to me then and I knew I couldn't stop the wheels of fate. It was fate and nothing else. This simply had to happen." She clutched me with a burst of affection she couldn't control. "I'm sorry the night is almost over. I hate the thought of going to bed alone. I hate the thought of eating breakfast with Jonathan in the morning. I hate everything that doesn't include you."

I couldn't say anything because I was asking myself a question I had tried to answer earlier in the night. How could things be like this when I was supposed to be in love with Dayne?

"Do you feel that way, too, Ches?"

"I feel that way too, darling."

"You called me darling."

"I mean it."

"Then you love me, too." She sat up and caught me by the shoulders.

I sighed heavily. "Let me get things straight in my mind, Verna. I can't even think now."

She nodded wisely and a satisfied smile came to her lips. "I won't push you. Not with words, anyhow." She came close to me and kissed me and presently her weight came down on me. All of a sudden we were back at the little park and the world was whirling crazily out of its orbit and reality had fled.

Some minutes later I found myself holding her as though she were a shuddering kitten, her dress in delicious revealing disarray and her body as limp as death while her starved lungs tried to feed themselves.

Her eyes came up, misty and deep. "See what sort of persuasion I'm capable of?"

"I see," I said huskily and abandoned my foolish caution. "I love you, Verna. That's all I can say. I love you to the fullest my mind is capable of imagining. I love you with a completeness I felt only tonight."

She held me and cried softly for a while then looked up, her eyes aswim in twin baths of crystal. "I knew it, Ches. You had to love me. It couldn't have been anything else or I'd have known."

I thought for a while then said, "Now that it's settled, what comes next?"

She cuddled close. "Let's don't foul up this wonder with plans. Let's live a while then we can plan what we want to do."

"That is a unique attitude."

Her smile was catlike and relaxed. "Of course. Aren't I rather a unique girl?"

"There can be no argument with that," I said with a profundity I felt completely.

We got out in front of the hotel and had to ring for admittance at that late hour. In the lobby she squeezed my hand and made a kiss-mouth and disappeared up the 'short steps to the second floor while I went on into the elevator to the seventh floor.

Lonzo was snoring in one bed, Phil was wide awake doing something to a sheet of paper and the third bed beckoned to me invitingly.

"You are out all night making love while I slave," he complained, scratching one big toe with the other. He was clad in opulent pajamas that revealed the degree of excellence with which he had been put together. From neck to ankles he was a masculine dream in symmetry and I could tell by the long lean muscles that wreathed his body he would be a mean *hombre* to tangle with. He had a look of tense alertness even when relaxed, like a jungle cat that could snap into explosive action in a flash.

"I did all right," I mumbled, still numb from Verna's terrific voltage. "What happened after I left?"

"Well, about the time you departed the gentleman on the sidewalk joined his scabby ancestors. Naturally, he had nothing by way of identification. A search of the area revealed a parked car that tried to get away but the traffic in Merida isn't geared for speed and he piled into a two-wheeled cart and wrecked the car. The cart was unhurt as was the man when the police pulled him from the wreckage."

"So we have a live one for a change."

Phil shrugged. "Fat lot of good it'll do. He clammed up and we were unable to budge him short of a toe toasting which I deplore. We used their own tactics and shot him full of sodium amytal but he doesn't know but one thing."

"Which is?"

"He showed considerable fright when I asked him if he'd pilot me to Sierra Negro."

I nodded and lit a cigarette. "So what do we do now?"

"We commandeer a good cruiser. One has already been ordered. We take a trip tomorrow."

I felt washed out and useless. "Phil, I'm afraid the government wasted a lot of time and energy screening me for a job like this. I don't seem to be much good at it."

He made a broad gesture with his hands to indicate depreciation. "You were..." He hesitated and bent me a look that was sharp enough to cut. "You are under a difficult type of pressure. That and it being your first outing of this sort has you somewhat stymied. But I expect great things of you in the near future."

"I thought you said this was your first outing, too."

"Only as a white card man. I've done quite a lot of sneaking in my life. Did you ever read of an incident about eight months ago off Baja California that nearly caused an international disturbance?"

I sat up straight. I remembered it well enough because two unidentified guys in unidentified fighter planes had bombed two of Russia's biggest freighters to the bottom of the Pacific. They had enough of some chemical or ore to send their atomic research ahead by years, something that is quite rare and found in about three places in the world. Also there had been a guy by the name of—I sat straighter still. Phillipe Mendoza!

I grinned. "You're modest, anyhow. I'll give you that. The great Phil Mendoza, flying bearcat of the RAF, who flew Norcross into Yugoslavia, who shot down a slue of Messerschmidts and Stukas, who climbed out of every prison camp in Germany. How come the alias?"

He shrugged. "The family was against it and so was the government until they got into the fracas. I flew wing with the present president of Mexico. He wasn't president then but a bird who wanted fighting wings. There were several of us over there. We didn't do badly."

CHAPTER EIGHT

I THINK I got about two hours sleep that night and was awakened by Verna on the phone at six-thirty.

"Wake up," she said in a sparkling voice. "I've had early coffee and walked to the market place. Now I'm ready for breakfast. I don't want to eat with Jonathan."

"What does Jonathan have to say about it?"

"He's terribly miffed and says he's going home."

"Huh! Let him go home. I'll still be around."

"Going to eat with me?"

"Sure. Be down in thirty minutes."

I darted for the bath only to find that Phil was already there, his face loaded with lather. "Step it up," I said. "I got a date for breakfast."

"Don't let it extend past eight o'clock," he mumbled through the lather. "We have a date with a sea-going cruiser at Progresso as soon as we can get there."

"How shall I dress?" I asked.

"Khakis or dungarees. People aren't formal down here. They dress for comfort. Yucatan is the Louisiana of Mexico." That from the Beau Brummel of Mexico!

I dug out some khakis that had been well-pressed and they didn't look half bad. On top I wore a green *guayabera* that Lonzo had bought for me the day before.

I finally got shaved and made it to the lobby where Verna greeted me in a cool mint green dress of cotton that fitted better than the previous creation had, if such is possible. Around her head, keeping tendrils of soft brown hair out of her eyes, was a ribbon of the same color. She bounced up and caught me by both hands. "You don't know how hard it is to keep from bussing you right here in front of Don Fernando and everybody."

I took a quick look over my shoulder and if the knowing look in Don Fernando's eyes meant anything we might as well have gone ahead. What he missed in the realm of human reaction wouldn't be worth worrying about if I was any judge. He smiled and walked over. "I am about to eat breakfast. I beg that you be my guests—on second thought I'm afraid I shall have to ask your pardon. It seems that my son desires my presence." He bowed and walked away but I didn't see Fernando, Junior.

I looked accusingly at her. "Did you let disappointment flit over your face when he asked us to breakfast?"

"I did not! I should have been delighted. He's cute."

"Well, he must have thought he saw it. He's a little too sharp for comfort."

"I'm hungry!" she said forcefully. "Maybe we can finish before Jonathan comes down. He's a mattress-back."

We sat and ordered tall cold glasses of orange juice, papaya chilled so that it hurt our teeth, and mounds of golden scrambled eggs, bacon and coffee.

"Have you seen Jonathan since last night?"

"No. He was waiting up when I came in. He spouted a lot of stuff and all I did was grin at him. He went back to his room in a rage, threatening to leave. Sometimes he's a queer egg."

"Do you think he will go home?"

"I hope he does and that's as far as I'll go."

"I've got to leave today. I don't know how long it'll take."

"Oh." She caught her breath and her face fell. "I was hoping we could go to Tulipanes again tonight."

A chill went over me as last night unreeled quickly through my mind. "That'd be swell but we no can do, probably. I'm sorry, Verna, but I can't tell you anything about this business. It's confidential as all hell and I'm following Soldarez around like a dog on a leash. Maybe we'll be back early and maybe we won't. I just don't know."

"It's all right," she said with a smile. "Women shouldn't question men about their dark secrets, anyhow. Still love me?"

"Too much for comfort. And you?"

Her eyes grew soft and a little twist came to the corners of her mouth. "Oh, Ches. How can I tell you when it's too big for me?"

"Look out, you'll spoil your breakfast."

She started making circles in the table cloth with a knife handle. "I almost have already. Do you think Jonathan will go home?"

"Can't say. There he comes. Maybe he'll tell us himself."

Jonathan, his bright blond hair standing on end and his eyes hard, made straight for the table. "Since Verna is obviously out of her mind I'll have to deal directly with you—whoever you are. I forbid you to see her again."

I looked at him for a moment. "Is that a fact? Well, now I do declare. Beat it before I slap you silly with a tortilla. I think Verna's choice of men is impeccable."

"And I think it's unsanitary. I've warned you."

"Okay, you've warned me, so beat it."

He turned red but he spun about and left, whereupon I turned back to my breakfast and finished it while Verna looked detachedly into the near distance.

"Is this going to get you in trouble at home?" I asked.

She chuckled grimly. "All sorts of trouble but I've just decided something. I was thinking of that when you spoke. So what? I have an expensive education and what if I do get the heave-ho? A lot of girls make their own living. Peace can cost too much, you know, and I think I've just come to understand that."

After breakfast I joined Phil and we entaxied for Progresso, making the twenty-mile trip without incident. Progresso has a good harbor with wide sandy beaches extending for miles on either side. It handles most of the seagoing traffic for the Yucatan Peninsula and at least one seafaring man had a good boat. It was a fifty-foot sea-going cruiser that had been outfitted for luxurious living; but it was still fast.

As we boarded her I asked Phil, "How far is this place?"

"About a hundred miles, a few more or less. We can make it in four of five hours. Think we have enough reinforcements?"

I looked where he pointed and saw the man he had detailed to watch me last night leading a group of ten of the solidest Mayans I ever saw. They were short but their shoulders were tremendous and they carried short carbines with a familiarity that didn't suggest lack of knowledge of their weapons. They wore green *guayaberas* and green cotton trousers. Their feet were shod with flexible strap sandles.

"Where did they come from?"

"Montejo put me onto them. I could have gotten men from him but it would have taken time and red tape and I'm afraid time is somewhat of the essence. He has used them on several critical occasions and swears by them. What did you do with Lonzo?"

"I left him to ogle the señoritas in the market and generally disport himself. Lonzo is a man of peace unless you get him cornered. Who was my bodyguard last night?"

"He's priceless. He's from my home and I've used him plenty."

For four hours and fifty minutes we rode the blue waters of the Gulf and gradually crept up on Sierra Negro, an island that reared itself out of the water like a black mushroom with sheer rocky sides and sandy beaches as white as the rock was black.

"The beaches look good but actually they are very narrow. I've wondered how they got there at all. The water is very deep."

"Where do we drop anchor?"

He pointed. "There's a small inlet where you see the white water. We will enter and drop anchor where the water's calm."

Twenty minutes later we came to a stop and the cruiser swung around on its hawser. They dropped two dinghies and soon we were standing on a narrow little ledge of rock that was mostly bird droppings and debris of all sorts.

"Maybe I'm thick," I said, "but what does this get us?"

"You'll see," said Phil. He belted on his gun over white coveralls that managed to fit him as well as his uniform, then shot a streak of rapid speech at his man who in turn gave orders to the Mayans. We walked a hundred yards along the ledge and finally reached a place that showed signs of man. The ledge had been utilized as a wharf and the area was clean and worn.

"I don't like it," said Phil, his agate eyes narrowing as he swept every inch of visible terrain.

"What don't you like?"

"The signs show they've been here very recently, but that's all. No boats and no signs but signs."

"Do you know the place?"

"I've talked to a man who does. Let's go."

We walked about thirty yards further and ducked through a crack in the wall of rock and found ourselves in a cave of truly titanic dimensions. The roof was not stalagmited or stalactited—whichever is which—as I would have expected, but just black volcanic rock. There were two openings overhead that let in quite a lot of light.

We spent a couple of hours exploring but found nothing but a lot of signs of recent occupancy. At the furthest distance from the first entrance was another opening but it was low and served to let the water in to make a big glassy pool.

Phil pointed. "I'd like to know what's at the bottom of that." He spoke Spanish to his man who held a conference with the Mayans and came forward with a stocky son of Yucatan and another conference was held.

"The water isn't too deep here," said Phil. "This man says he's a good diver so we'll see what he can find on the bottom."

They rigged a stout rope with a boulder to carry it down and as soon as it had struck bottom at about thirty feet the Mayan, stripped to a bit of sisal cord holding a sharp knife around his waist, grabbed the rope and slid into the depths. I nearly strangled before he reappeared with a broad grin on his face and spit out a story in breathless Spanish.

"He claims he's found a great archeological discovery," said Phil and ordered the men to pull up the rope. They labored mightily—until a perfectly carved stone statue came to the surface and was soon sitting on the dry rock, dripping unconcernedly.

Phil's eyes were narrowed and he began to massage his chin.

"What is it?" I asked.

"It is a *Chaac-Mool*," he said slowly, "and it has no business here."

"Why?"

"Because they are only found in Chichen-Itza." He reached over and tapped it with a heavy silver ring and the apparently dead stone rang like a bell. The natives ceased their chatter and stared at the thing through wide eyes. Then the diver launched into a loud harangue that lasted three minutes.

"He says," translated Phil, "that there is only one other *Chaac-Mool* that rings and it is in the House of a Thousand Columns at Chichen. Maybe we have found something—Hell!" Phil is not a man at using hard words but he sure ripped that "Hell" out strong. He bent forward and with a pen knife cut a thin but stout sisal cord from the statue's neck. We hadn't noticed it because of the discoloration. "There goes the archeological find," muttered Phil. "I was beginning to feel as excited as the Indian but this kills it."

"Why?" I asked.

"Because it's been used for something. Maybe to weigh something down as a sinker of some sort."

"Wasn't there anything else down there?"

"The diver says not and he's good." He pushed his cap back on his head and stared at the thing for a moment then asked the diver something. The man answered.

Phil said, "I never saw a *Chaac-Mool* in this state. It looks actually new. The native says he never saw one this new either. Well, it looks like this is either the reddest herring I ever saw or a lead that'll take us to Chichen-Iza. Just what or who I expect to find there, I can't say. I can say that I'm sick at the results of this. I had hung quite a lot on this angle and what do I get but a statue new or a thousand years old. At any rate the museum at Merida will be glad to have it so we'll take it along." After another tedious search that netted nothing we put the *Chaac-Mool* aboard and headed back for Progresso. Halfway back in the gathering dusk something like the projectile out of a gun whammed over our heads and was soon lost in the distance. None of us got a decent look at it and all we made out was a trail of fire that in a matter of seconds had winked out in the distance.

I found Phil in the stem trying vainly to locate it through a pair of powerful binoculars.

"What was it," I asked, "a flying saucer?"

"Could have been," he said with an outraged grunt. "In fact, nothing will surprise me now. However, if it was they're powering saucers with a ram jet. I don't think I could mistake that sound."

Progresso winked at us in the distance finally and I began to wonder if Verna had gone to bed.

We sweated the statue ashore and left it in charge of one of the port officials who promised to treat it like an eye in his head. That done we entaxied again for Merida.

Verna was waiting for me as I suspected she would be, but Phil crisply told me I'd better put it to bed since we would be leaving for Chichen in the morning as soon as Don Fernando could get us started. I piloted Verna behind an enormous column and kissed her thoroughly, her reaction being reward enough for a job well done.

"Things are beginning to happen, Ches?"

"We don't know. We think so."

"You know, I don't think I saw enough of Chichen when I was there. I think I'll go back."

I kissed her again, making it better than the first one. "I'm going to depend on that."

In the room Lonzo was asleep as usual and Phil was sitting on the bed in his shorts, frowning at a wall.

"Problems?" I asked.

"In a manner of speaking. Why would anyone carry a *Chaac-Mool* nearly two hundred miles to sink something?"

"Maybe it was a package that was made up here and carried there. Maybe they wanted to take it, dump it and come right back without having to look for a suitable boulder. I didn't see any, by the way, that weighed as much as that statue did."

"You make a good point. Another thing. What would they have wanted to sink that had to be weighted down that heavily?"

"Well, you have me there. With all that open sea and sharks and what-not it wasn't a body. Wait—wouldn't the tide tear out of that cave like a mill race when it was falling?"

He smacked a hard tanned thigh. "You got it. Whatever they had in that shallow water they didn't want to lose in the tide and find in deep water where it would be next to impossible to retrieve."

"But what about that small line? That wasn't stout enough to hold any particular weight."

"Right, but I rather suspect the line was nothing more than a guide. They secreted one end under a rock and used it to find whatever was in the water. When they were through with it they just let it go and the line fouled on something and snapped." He moved a palm over his face. "I feel like a fool looking for international brigands in a dwarf jungle around pyramids and temples that have little interest save for tourists and archeologists. Something's wrong here and I don't know what it is."

I took off my *guayabera* and prepared to take a shower. "I'll give 'em one thing. They sure don't let their right hand know what their left is doing."

"Yes, and that makes it hard for us because they're looking down our throats. We don't know a thing and they know plenty. They're always a step ahead of us."

I took off my pants and threw them into a chair. "Tell me one thing. Do you believe this business is as serious as the Cheese seemed to think?"

He shrugged. "It's serious, all right. Whether it is serious as of now or merely something that could be serious eventually, we don't know. But the idea is sound. Imagine what a panic would ensue if the bottom would fall out from under two of the most intrinsically valuable commodities in world economy. I seriously doubt that these people have enough right now to start a panic. They do have a sure-fire method of getting more and they could soon be a threat, a real threat."

The phone tinkled and Phil lifted the receiver and spoke. His face grew as hard as oak and his eyes became just black flecks of onyx in his face as he listened. He said *"Gracias"* and hung up.

"Something?"

"Plenty. The liner *Delgado* en route from Rio to New Orleans with two million in bullion destined for Fort Knox was run aground off Trinidad through some error in navigation. As soon as the passengers were off the ship a sub came up and ordered the bullion into a lighter, else they'd torpedo the ship and take it anyway. The captain was hard-headed so he caught a Whitehead amidships and the ship settled onto the coral. He lost his ship as well as the bullion.

"Maybe they'll bring it here," I said excitedly.

He smiled tiredly. "Where?"

I thought for a second and had to grin, too. "Damn if I know."

"That's what we have to find out. It would hurt our pride if Norcross and the others beat us to this coup."

I shucked out of my drawers and started for the shower. "Your pride, son. Right now I feel like Ned in the Primer and I ain't got a lot of pride."

CHAPTER NINE

THE GIGANTIC *Castillo*, rearing its pyramidal bulk into the morning mists, gave me a quick chill as we rolled past the gate marking the entrance to the Chichen-Itza ruins. It was like getting a glimpse into a past so dim that it was only a memory carved in stone. It was a feeling that was to grow the longer I stayed around the place. The car rolled on past and into the grounds of the unbelievable Mayaland Hotel where more smiling attendants relieved us of our luggage and escorted us to our rooms. We came down to breakfast and after eating, as we sat drinking more coffee, I asked Phil: "What's the first move?"

He sighed heavily. "You ask a lot of questions. Why don't you answer some?"

"Because I'm the PFC in this outfit and I don't know from nothing. You're the boss and I expect bosses to tell me what to do."

"Go out and get shot," he said bad-temperedly.

"I almost did. Maybe I'll get the real thing. You can bury me in the Temple of the Warriors."

He lit a fragrant cigarette and emitted a cloud of blue smoke. "The first thing is to make a detailed visit of the ruins and familiarize ourselves with directions and the terrain. It wouldn't do to go wandering around some dark night and take a dive into one of the *cenotes*."

"That should be interesting. I never dove into a *cenote*."

"You kill me," he said sarcastically. "You must add that to your long list of accomplishments."

At that moment a breathless little man followed hard by two breathless women careened into the grounds and disappeared around a palm from us.

"There," he said, standing up to peer, "went three people frightened out of their wits. This interests me strangely. Some of the natives occasionally are given to seeing Yum Chaac after a load of *aquardiente* but a guide and two hard-legged women..."

In five minutes he came back trailed by a frightened guide and a policeman with a lugubrious face. "We have murder now," said Phil hissingly through his teeth, his hard eyes slitted with thought. "Let's go view the corpse."

We walked up the road to the main gate, entered and walked past the *Castillo* with a group of tourists snaking up its steep face, the only way you can climb it, past the Temple of the Eagles to the so-called Ball Court.

"In there, señor," said the nervous guide, pointing and not caring to go any further. Phil had other ideas, however, and he went anyhow.

The ball court has two steep stone walls running its length maybe forty yards apart. At either end is an imposing temple with sculptured pictures of various scenes. At the south end of the east wall is a knockout of a temple with gigantic snakes guarding the entrance.

On either side of the field are tremendous stone rings said to be goals, the object of the game being to pass a ball of native gum through the rings. Some few authorities snort at the idea. We found these few to be right, speculatively at any rate.

The body lay on its face exactly between the two rings midway the court and Phil stopped as soon as he saw this. "Now what a positively unique place to find a body," he said softly.

"What's unique about it?" I asked.

"The exactitude with which it is placed in relation to the ball court, and, of course, the stone rings. Luis, frighten that dog away there."

Luis, the guide, hurled a stone at the cur who yelped and ran off a little way and stopped again. We walked up to the body and though we searched the area closely as well as the body we couldn't find any injury or any weapon that might have caused death.

"Nuts," I said, feeling let down. "He died of heart failure. How do you know he was murdered?"

Phil grinned. "That's the policeman in me. I didn't know it. I do now, though."

"Why?"

"He's the man they caught night before last in Merida. The one who tried to get away."

"Looks like he succeeded."

"Yes, but he didn't get far. Luis, run up to the hotel and see if you can find a doctor—and run that dog away. I mean completely away."

Luis picked up a handful of stones and hurled them hoping his scattergun effect might land a lucky shot on the cur. Then some strange things happened. One stone flying wild struck the east ring and a sound came from it that we could feel deep in our belly; we didn't actually hear anything but our eardrums vibrated like mad. The dog absolutely went into convulsions. It fell out on the grass and rolled around, foam flecked its lips and its eyes rolled wildly. All the while you would have thought it was being roasted alive from the anguished yelps that came from its throat. Finally it stopped, lay still for a while, then sat up slowly and laboriously like a drunk crawling out of a gutter.

The policeman went white and mumbled something that sounded like *"Madre de Dios."*

Luis stood stunned and uncomprehending while Phil began to massage his jaw. "How very damn peculiar," he said half to himself. "Luis, get a stick and strike that ring again."

"Your excellency," begged Luis sweating profusely, "I think I should get the doctor, don't you? I crave your pardon a thousand times, but I dare not touch that ring."

Phil shrugged. "Very well. Get the doctor."

Luis left at a dead run while the policeman muttered that he was the one to go since he was much fleeter of foot than Luis.

Phil looked at him contemptuously, opened his mouth to order the policeman, shrugged and picked up a branch that lay nearby. Climbing the ramp that ran below the ring the whole width of the field, he reached up and smote the ring a smart blow. He fell backward as though a giant hand had struck him, full length on the grass and the dog went into another fit. Phil recovered before the dog did and walked back to us. "That is the most remarkable phenomena I think I ever witnessed," he said with the profundity of a man convinced beyond any shaking. "Was it like the first one?"

I nodded. "Just about. I could feel it way down and it made my ears tickle."

The dog had enough and as soon as he could command his reflexes he left the place, although he staggered somewhat.

Phil was marking the outline of the man in the earth with a little metal pencil he had taken from his pocket when he ran into something hard. He stopped and looked at the policeman and asked him something in Spanish. The man shrugged distractedly and looked the way Luis had gone. He was very desirous of following the example of the guide or the dog.

"This should be earth if the ball court idea is right," said Phil, "but I find stone here."

"Could be one of the dislodged blocks," I pointed out.

He nodded slowly. "Very likely. However, I'm going to find out."

He finished his outline and when he was done a jeep rolled up and stopped at the southeast opening wall. A little wisp of a man got out and started in our direction but Luis, in the jeep, stayed put. He didn't want any more of the same.

The little man dressed in cheap blue slacks and a white sport shirt might have weighed a hundred pounds but not much more. His body, face and arms were covered with dried yellow parchment-like skin and on his face it had stretched so tight he looked compressed. His hair was very black but sparse and unruly and his eyes were dark brown and given to watering.

"Trouble," he asked in a scratchy voice.

"Yes," said Phil. He introduced us and asked. "Are you a medical doctor, Dr. Moffet?"

The little man casually surveyed the body. "Yes," he said with a chuckle. "I was once. I'm now retired and have for some years devoted my time to my hobby, studying the ancient Mayans."

"See if you can tell me what the cause of death is here."

He stooped over the body and ran his fingers over the skull, neck and wrists. "I'm afraid it will not be possible until he is undressed and if that is done then it should be done in a laboratory where a complete post-mortem can be performed. The body is cold and certainly dead, but as to the cause it would take a more detailed examination. I suggest that he be taken to Merida."

Well, I lazed around that day with Verna, who had come to Chichen not too far behind us. The body had been sent to Merida and, except for taking leisurely visits to the various ruins, there was little else to do.

The doctor attached himself to us and followed us around explaining this and that in more detail than I cared to hear but we couldn't be rude to the little fellow. His presence, however, was discommoding, expecially since Verna was dressed in shorts and halter and didn't mind sneaking in low blows when Dr. Moffet's back was turned.

That night after an excellent dinner that a stevedore would have enjoyed, I got the shock of my young life. A waiter brought me an unsigned note asking me to come to room twenty. It was in a feminine hand and couldn't be from Verna because she was across the table from me and hadn't paid too much attention to the waiter.

"So," Verna was saying, "Jonathan threatened to go home again. I told him to go ahead because I was following you to Chichen. So he may be back in New Orleans by now giving a highly colored picture of my downfall to all hands."

I stood up. "Hang on for a few minutes. I have to go to the little boy's room."

She eyed a belt she had given me earlier that day, a hand-worked leather affair with a buckle of heavy silver that you could have brained someone with. "Run along," she said, stretching provocatively. "I have my belt on you now, in lieu of a ball and chain."

I left and in a few minutes knocked on the door of the room marked twenty. Dayne opened the door. I didn't fall on my face but I felt like it. She wore a pale blue creation that might be called a negligee but was so thin that the exciting pinkness of her skin showed through as well as the white boundaries of her briefs.

With a sob she fell into my arms and I, man that I am, couldn't resist. We stayed in the clinch until I began to get dizzy; then I picked her up and placed her on the bed.

"All right," I said in an attempt to go into a hard act. "Start talking."

She cried for a while then came under control. "You don't know how bitterly sorry I am, Ches, but please believe me I didn't have anything to do with it."

"Who beside you could have slipped a mickey into my drink and why wasn't yours drugged, too?"

"It's such a long sordid story," she said, her eyes filling again. "And I need your love so badly and there's very little time."

"Why?"

She shook her head. "I can't tell you now. Will you meet me at the top of the *Castillo* in the morning, early?"

"Yes. Did you or did you not put a mickey in my drink? At least you can tell me that."

"I did not. They were in the other part of the apartment and slipped into the kitchen." She threw herself into my arms and somehow the negligee just disappeared and she was nude save for the white briefs; then they were gone and she was a hot succulent fruit damp from being freshly peeled and her lips were driving me crazy. Then it seemed that I was driving her crazy.

"Oh, God, Ches…how…I've needed…you. Give me all your love in one great…" She gasped for breath and the rhythm seemed to falter them start anew. "…big bundle…wrap me in it…love me, Ches…hurt me…*love me.*"

I made it back eventually and it didn't take Verna long to know that something rather titanic had happened to me. Luckily she didn't know all the details.

"You look like you've seen and been wrestling with a ghost," she opined with one thick brown eyebrow raised.

"I have," I told her the truth, all of it that I could and she surprised me by understanding, or at any rate she didn't make a scene.

"I guess this had to happen," she said gently. "Now you can put us on the scales and weigh us under the same atmospheric conditions."

"That's a delightful thought," I mumbled. "I think I'm going to bed."

"That's a good idea, although it wasn't a few minutes ago."

"Now don't get sore," I protested.

"I'm not sore. There's a weight on my chest and I don't feel happy any more."

I didn't feel very happy about that time either. Get yourself lined up between two beautiful women, unable to escape either, and you'll see what I mean.

Phil came in about nine o'clock looking unhappy. "Someone," he began, taking off his blouse, "knows a lot more about Mayan lore than he should."

"Like what?"

"Like the fact that a man standing where that one was would be killed by sound waves coming from those stone rings."

"Damn," I said, sifting up in bed. "That's what killed him?"

"They can't find a wound. He had been tied, too. There were a few fibres of henequin on his clothes."

"How'd he get out of jail?"

"He flew between the bars," he sneered. "That's the way it looks. No one knows anything—more truthfully, is saying anything. That night he was there. The next morning he wasn't. The door to his cell was locked but the bird had flown, to coin a phrase."

"By the way," I said casually, "Dayne's in the hotel. Room twenty."

"So!" He raised his eyebrows. "Well, now, that's nice and cozy. What'd she have to say."

"She's been needing my love."

"Humph! Slip you a drugged drink again?"

"She says the bad people did that, then came in on us. She's going to tell me the story in full at the top of the *Castillo* in the morning."

"That's a nice breezy private place. Why there?"

"For the reasons you mentioned, very likely. She gave me the impression of being quite frightened."

"That shouldn't be hard for her to do." He hefted my belt and examined it. "Where'd you get this monstrosity?"

"Verna gave it to me."

He tossed it down and began to pull his shoes off. "What was the cause of death of our corpse?" I asked.

"Cerebral hemorrhage. His brains were a mass of blood but he hadn't been struck by anything. High frequency sound waves."

"They didn't kill us," I pointed out.

"That bothers me," he admitted. "They didn't kill the dog either but they gave him fits. I'm stuck with that theory and I'll hold onto it until I discover a better one."

"Why don't you ask the doctor?"

"For reasons of caution. I don't know him and although he's been around some time no one seems to know where he came from or anything about him."

"He's full of lore," I said. "He goes along with the ball court theory."

"Most people do because it's an easy explanation and looks feasible to the untrained eye. There are several ball courts but note one thing. They are all different sizes and have only one thing in common. The acoustic effects."

"What is your theory?"

"My theory is that each is an elaborate execution chamber in which enemies or people who had displeased the gods were put to death."

I nodded. "That's all right but for one thing. There are carvings depicting a man beheading another with a stone knife. What's the matter with that as a means of execution?"

"Nothing, of course, but beheading might have been deemed meet and fitting for a mere worker or common man. What about nobles or priests or generals of a beaten army? I don't claim infallability for this idea but it's an idea."

"Looks like they went to very great lengths to kill in a fancy manner."

"Someone did the same thing last night. Why didn't they just throw the victim in the *cenote* after banging him on the head? There are too many questions and not enough answers."

"All the scenes of executions I've seen in the carvings use an obsidian knife with a couple of people holding the culprit."

"I have a theory about that, too. They aren't executing the man—they're operating on him. Most people to be executed are bound, not held. You can see the same things in Egyptian sculpture and they are readable as doctors operating on a man."

"That makes sense," I said. "Suppose we sleep on it."

"I want to find out what that stone is I ran into this morning. I also want Luis to find me a dog."

"Better get that lad I met yesterday, José something or other. I don't think he's as impressed with ancient doings as Luis."

"See him for me, will you? I'm so loaded with plans and ideas I can't think properly."

The next morning was a memorable one for several reasons which I shall detail as I go along. True to my promise I went to the top of the *Castillo* which was still hidden in mist. It seemed eerie as hell waiting on an edifice constructed by hands long since turned to dust, standing in fog so thick the bottom had disappeared.

True to her promise, Dayne was there, but I wasn't prepared for this new version of her. She was clad in tailored blue slacks and a turtle neck sweater that showed her off the way I liked.

She kissed me and stood back, her eyes slitted and calculating; then with a smooth motion she drew a tiny pistol and let me have it, right in the guts. A boiling wave of agony went through me and I went down, a thin scream coming from somewhere and I remember wondering if it was me.

I came to propped against a smooth rock surface with Verna massaging my wrists and Phil Soldarez cursing like a pirate in Spanish.

"Am I dead?" I asked muzzily.

"No," he snapped. "No thanks to you. Verna here saved you on two counts. Your belt buckle turned that small bullet and Verna took care of Dayne before she could shove you over the side."

"Took care…" The mist had cleared and I stood up to see a group of people collected around something pretty shapeless below.

I shuddered and turned to Phil, "Tell me."

"She was here when Dayne arrived. She likes the *Castillo* in the mist. Verna came first and hid when she saw Dayne. Then you came. When she shot you and you fell, Verna pushed her over the side just as she was about to make up for the belt buckle's protection by sending you on a long roll. She's rather thoroughly dead, I'd say, although I haven't seen her. Those stone steps must have made hamburger of her. Poetic justice, as it were."

I pulled Verna to me and gave her a long soul-reaching kiss. "Now let's get the hell down from here!"

Dayne was not a pretty sight. It is doubtful that she had a whole bone in her body and her face was just jelly. Dr. Moffet was there but shrugging his shoulders. "There's nothing to be done. She was dead halfway down."

That was that and all I had was a belly that felt like a host of hornets had stung it.

José Mercader, the lad I had mentioned to Phil, was willing and even eager. Furthermore, he could speak good English. He caught a small cur and put a leash on it and the four of us went to the Ball Court, while members of the local constabulary took care of all that remained of Dayne. I felt a twinge of sadness about her because I hate to see beauty die, no matter what it had been. Verna respected my mood and said nothing as we walked along.

Phil, measuring with his eye, pegged the dog in the center of the diagram of the dead man's body so as to make the test as exact as possible.

"Now, José, if you will be so kind as to go over and tap the stone ring..."

"Hold it," I said. "Let him throw a rock. That thing knocked you flat. It might blow José clean away."

"That's right. Think you can hit it with a rock, José?"

"Yes, señor. There are plenty of rocks so I can throw until I do hit it."

It took him five rocks to make it and though he caught the ring a solid blow and we were pretty well vibrated, the cur didn't do a thing but yawn.

"That does it," snarled Phil. "The other dog just had well-timed natural fits if any sort of fits can be termed natural. The whole carefully constructed theory is without bottom."

"Just the same," I said, "I want another trial. I don't have your fulminating Latin attitude. Get to throwing, José." I unpegged the dog and led him to the approximate spot where the other one had gone crazy, then I pegged the leash into the grass and went back to Phil and Verna. The third try was good and the dog went insane. He had more stamina and guts than the other one and instead of rolling around without purpose or gain; after a couple of rolls he came to his feet, jerked the leash out of the ground and set sail like a cat boat in a hurricane.

"This fulminating Latin begs the phlegmatic Anglo-Saxon's pardon," said Phil as we left the place, "and the theory still stands although a little weaker. That place is a problem in acoustics. José, can we borrow a shovel?"

"I think so, although an attendant will probably want to be present in case you unearth treasure of any sort and try to take it away."

"He's welcome and can even do the digging if he wants to."

That afternoon, after twenty minutes of digging, we all stood and admired the sacrificial altar or death seat. It was lyre-shaped with prongs below the arm rests and where the legs would have been. "Like I said," said Phil, exultantly. "They bound people to be killed." The seat wasn't moved but left exactly where it had been. "José, bring the dog."

José brought a dog but it was another one. "Our first one was nowhere to be found," he said apologetically. "This one is quite old and useless."

"He may be a martyr to an ancient science," said Verna, "but I still don't like it."

"Neither do I," said Phil, "but this is very important. José, ring the bell."

José was getting better and hit the ring the first throw. But nothing happened and Phil damned under his breath, his theory tottering again.

"Look," I said. "We're only using one ring. Maybe the other one is lethal, too."

We tried it with no better results; then Phil had an idea. "José, go plunder around until you can find two long sticks. You and I will try to strike the rings simultaneously from the top of the wall."

"You're an ass if you try that," I said. "You might get knocked off that place."

"You and the attendant will sit on our legs," he said, so José went searching for the sticks. After fifteen minutes or thereabouts he came back with two green saplings long enough to reach the rings from the top. Phil and I went to the east ring, leaving the west one to José and the attendant, whose name was Fango or something like that. Phil made the agreed signal and they tapped the rings together. My hair seemed to stand on end from the shock and Phil blacked out momentarily.

José's helper, Fango, let go a yell and departed under forced draft, leaving José a limp heap on the wall. He came back about as quickly as Phil did and grinned weakly at us across the field. The dog was a still silent figure on the stone seat.

Verna, who had been standing almost against the south temple, came forward holding her ears. "My God, what a noise. Like all the trains in the world in a head-on collision."

Phil's jaw dropped and I stared. "Sound?" He ejaculated. "We didn't hear a thing."

She gaped at us like we were fools then said. "Let's get out of here. I don't like it."

We examined the dog, and found not a hair disturbed. But I think every blood vessel in his body had burst, making him look like a red sausage. Phil straightened up, his lips grim. "Well, that's all the experimenting necessary. I wonder what else these people know that we don't."

"I found something," said José, "when I was looking for the sticks."

"What?" I asked.

"A hole covered with bushes to give the impression that it is not used."

"Let's go," said Phil exultantly.

"Hold it," I said, feeling that at last I had contributed something to the game. "Maybe we are watched and if we are they'll know we've found it. Maybe it isn't important, but then again, maybe it is."

"You're right," he said shamefacedly. "José, not a word to anyone, hear?"

"No, señor. I suggest, too, that I find Fango and silence him. I gather you're not too keen to have this business spoken about."

"A topping idea," said Phil. "Tell him it'll go hard with him if he breathes a word—if he hasn't already." José departed at a run with Phil watching him keenly. "That boy is wasted here. He's sharp."

"Make him one of your gunsels," I said.

"I was thinking of that," he replied.

It was an hour before lunch and we were sitting in our room drinking as taste-tingling a martini as I ever had my claws on. "This," said Verna, making herself seductive and lovely on my bed with a drink in her hand, clad in blue toreador pants and a white T-shirt, "is the life. I love these piney things."

Phil grunted. "I'm glad someone around here can enjoy life. I feel like a Chicago rail yard with trains running through my head. Ches, let's rehash a bit. Dayne was with them hand and glove all the time, right?"

"Looks like it Tell me something—why did she try to push me off the *Castillo*?"

"So you'd appear to have fallen," said Verna. "That little bullet hole would have been lost in the ... er, shuffle."

Phil smiled. "Thanks, my dear. Ordinarily I have to do all the thinking. Dayne's attempt failed. We have a murder of one of their men obviously done by them. Why?"

"It got back to them that he reacted when you mentioned ..."

"Hold it. I know what you mean. Pardon us, Verna, but we're going to have to talk over your head or run you out."

"Talk ahead," she said. "I don't want to know your old secrets anyway."

"All right," continued Phil. "Maybe that's why they did him in. Why pick the place they did?"

"You have me there," I said. "I agree that there should have been a better place. The *cenote*, as you said. Any damn place but one of the plushest ruins on the course."

He frowned for a moment. "Still they had a point. How was he murdered? By the sheerest accident we discovered it. That was the one safe thing about it. No one could have proved that he was murdered if we hadn't lucked onto the secret. If they capture you and put you on that seat, Ches, object strenuously."

"I shall," I said sarcastically, "and I shall expect you to the rescue with guns blazing."

"I'll do my best. What do we do now? Wait for something else to happen?"

"I think it would be a good idea to sneak out and inspect the hole José found."

"A capital idea and one we shall follow, come dark."

"Me, too," said Verna. "I want to be near Ches when dark falls."

"Nope," I said firmly. That's out. You stay here."

She pouted but didn't offer any objections and we all trooped down to lunch only to be pounced upon by Dr. Moffett.

"Ah, Captain Soldarez, Mr. Markham and the lovely Miss Martell. May I impose my poor company on you? I abhor eating alone." We couldn't run him off so he joined us.

"I hear you've been conducting some interesting experiments at the Ball Court. I might say that the impact on the archeological world will be great. We were smug in our belief that they were ball courts and nothing more."

Phil nodded but didn't say anything.

"And that interesting object you excavated. How did you know it was there?"

"Accident. I was marking the outline of the body when I touched it. It was only just below the surface."

"Very, very interesting. I too felt vaguely that such an imposing edifice was a little overdone for a mere game."

"I've seen some bigger ones," said Verna. "The Sugar Bowl, for one."

"Quite, but the great stadia of the United States are utilitarian to a degree. This one was constructed at huge effort and is quite sumptuous." He sighed. "Every little mystery solved helps add to the store against the eventual day when we shall know all. I feel sure it is coming."

With what little I knew, I wasn't so sure. Maybe he would, but right now I'd settle for a little information on men who sank ships for gold bullion. So far we had an imposing array of incidents none of which seemed to bring us any closer.

Lunch passed with the doctor rambling deep into the obscurity of Mayan culture, possible origin and the like. After lunch Verna cornered me; I had been left high and dry by Phil who had just disappeared.

"Let's go see the Nunnery, Ches. I never get enough of that place."

"It doesn't seem to bother you that you shoved a human being to death this morning."

Her face went blank. "Should it? She was about to kill you."

I squeezed her hand. "No. I keep forgetting that you're not like other people. Forget I said it."

CHAPTER TEN

THE NUNNERY is a vast pile that has to be climbed and at one o'clock it can be hot in Yucatan.

We made it to the top and in a little protected alcove Verna promptly came into my arms; the heat rose steadily until we were both shivering. She had changed to a green cotton dress with a flared skirt that opened down the front and she was apparently feeling her freedom because she had worn no bra. I let her down easily on a clean wind-swept ledge and then my questing hand found that she had worn nothing except the dress and a half-slip. She slid easily out of them both and there on the top of the world two people blended in nature's mightiest performance. She was smooth and hot and rhythmic and her arms were as powerful as a man's. Her legs twined and gripped like twin serpents, creamy tan and lovely beyond words—yet so strong.

It came, smote us like a bolt of lightning and left us drenched with sweat but drifting in a haze that is unsurpassable. She clung to me, her breath coming in soft whimpers, burying her face in my neck, muttering endearing phrases that made no sense but could not be mistaken.

She sat up and looked down on me, a sweet smile coming to her face. "Ches, I love you so much."

"I can return that with interest," I said profoundly.

"Just since this morning?"

"No. This morning just drove the final nail. I wonder how your family is going to react."

❧ ❧ ❧

It was a grim-faced Soldarez who presented himself to us that afternoon as we lazed in the bar sipping *Carta Clara.* "Come up to the room," he said tightly, ignoring Verna, a matter that told plenty in itself. Phil was not a man to ignore lovely women under usual circumstances.

Then I noticed that the off side of his face had been bandaged. I didn't say anything but got up and followed him.

He closed the door behind us and motioned to a seat. "Up till this moment I think we've been just a shade casual about this thing. I shall endeavor now to point out that even a shade of casualness is likely to reap us six feet of sod and a slab of marble appropriately inscribed."

"Trouble today?" I asked, looking at the bandage.

"I went on a little tour that I had in mind and I got Luis to take me in the hotel jeep. A bullet fired at considerable range missed me by the merest whisker. The cut is from a piece of the windshield glass." He pulled back the neck of his blouse and showed me the dark streak on his stiff collar that had been made by the passage of the bullet. A whisker was right. One inch closer and he would have spouted blood like a blowing whale.

"We went around a slight curve about a mile from here and the shot came through the windshield. The only likely cover was a small rocky ridge three hundred yards away. Evidently they are weary of failure and have found some top grade help or else they're doing their own dirty work."

"Some of their previous help wasn't too hot," I pointed out.

"Very true and I think the reason is simple. They were just men working for hire. The head men didn't want any of their own men caught for good reason. There are many ways to make a man reveal secrets."

"You don't have to tell me," I said. "They could have had everything I knew for the asking when they had me loaded with that drug."

Phil compressed his hands into a ball and strained until the cords stood out on his wrists. "The point of getting you here is to tell you that from now on we're sitting ducks. They know us and we don't know them. Dayne, for example. Until she pulled that gun and let you have it you still thought she was a misused gal who was all right deep down. What do you know of Verna?"

"Oh, hell," I protested. "She was swimming in a pool when I first saw her trying to fend off Jonathan's attentions."

"Yet she walked through the lobby, saw you and thereupon fell like a ton of bricks. What is this fatal attraction you have for women?"

"Dayne met me on purpose. Verna met me by accident."

"Is that so? How do you know the accident wasn't on purpose?"

"Well..." He had me there. "I don't know it, of course, but—well, Verna's okay. She saved my life."

His grin was so sarcastic it almost amounted to an insult. "I'm not impressed," he said gently. "But I suppose that by now things have come to the point of no return. Just be careful and when you're inclined to go overboard remember Dayne who, if I'm not mistaken, had you in a similar spot."

I blushed, of course, and he chuckled. "We're both too young to be greatly impressed by death but the young are no less dead than the aged when that state arrives. Remember it and remember that every time you poke your head out of doors you might be met with a bullet."

It was growing dark and in spite of the pressure of the situation I was hungry so we went down and had roast pheasant and a lot of trimmings, washed down by a dry white wine recommended by the waiter. Verna was present but silent and we ate with our minds on various angles of recent happenings. We were drinking coffee when Don Fernando came up to the table and bowed courteously to Phil. "I ask your pardon, Captain Soldarez, but I have a rather upsetting personal problem I should like to discuss with you."

Phil, who was on his feet instantly, bowed no less courteously and asked in Spanish, "Is it something my friends should not know?"

"Hardly." Don Fernando spoke English again.

"In that case suppose you join us at coffee and tell us about it."

The courtly gentleman sat and massaged his hands together nervously. "Possibly all of you listening might be better than one. It is in regard to the unfortunate occurrence, the murder. Frankly, I am concerned about the effect it may have on the hotel, the tourists and, as a matter of course, my business."

Phil nodded. "Understandable, but I think you need have no worry. Your servants and staff are not involved unless by the sheerest freak of chance. Their conduct has been exemplary and nothing untoward attaches to them. I regret, Don Fernando, that Señor Markham and I cannot discuss the nature of our business here but please believe me when I say that it is of vast importance, not just to you or me or Yucatan or Chichen, but to the world. It is unfortunate that we should find it centered here but it is not we who determined it. I hope that we can bring it to a speedy and satisfactory conclusion. I assure you that in no way will your hotel or name suffer. In fact, when it all comes into the open, Chichen and Yucatan will be the center of world attention. People will know of it and visit here who never heard of it before. It is my sincere belief that the effects will be highly beneficial. Another point is our discovery of the use to which the rings of the Ball Court were used. That is new. If a stone jar or glass should be placed in the sacrificial or execution chair and the rings struck simultaneously, I feel certain that it will be shivered to fragments. The chair is solid and takes no damage. Think what a feat to perform before tourists and the effects on them."

Don Fernando, instead of looking pleased about the Ball Court affair, looked a little let down. "Forgive me, Captain, but I'm afraid the guides and certain of our visitors will be more impressed than I with the phenomena. I am always a little disappointed, although I know I shouldn't be, when visitors do not appreciate the vast antiquity, the immense mysteries that surround this place. To me it is something very nearly sacred, not merely a curiosity or a juggler's stage."

Phil grinned. "Just the same, there are people like those you mention. We can't all be addicts of archeology."

Don Fernando stood up. "My thanks for listening to my problem. As you say, all might be well. The fact that your father and I are old friends, Captain, lends great weight to your assurances. I have the fondest remembrances of Don Hermano and to know him is to know his children."

Phil stood up also. "Your words are most kind and I shall repeat them to my father."

Don Fernando left then and we sat in silence for a moment; then Phil said, "I share Don Fernando's concern but for a different reason. I am a man accustomed to dealing with facts and evidence. At the moment I have very few of the former and none of the latter. Dayne might have told us something because I think she was the first outward effort from within the charmed circle. The others knew nothing. We either have dead people or people who are mere tools. It is discouraging, to say the least."

"We have a little trip to make," I reminded him, "and I don't think we're dressed for it."

"Where is that?" asked Verna.

"Secret," I said.

"You're going into that hole."

"And you're staying right here," I told her commandingly.

"Well, maybe I'll stay but I won't like it."

"That is a matter of lesser importance. Your neck is too lovely to endanger. Let's go, Phil."

We dressed in dark dungarees and armed ourselves well. I wore a .45 in my belt under my dungaree jacket and Phil wore his some place I couldn't see. He used the phone for a moment and then we left. Passing the *Castillo* we were joined by Pepe and his silent troop of men looking like green-clad gnomes—except that their brawny shoulders were too broad for gnomes and their stride too graceful.

"We're taking them?"

He shook his head. "No. They're waiting on guard outside. I'm not walking into a trap if I can help it."

"You were all ready to steal my hole," said a voice at my elbow. "Remember, I found it." It was José carrying a machete that looked sharp enough to behead someone.

"There might be danger," pointed out Phil.

"No more to me than to you, Captain, or Señor Markham."

"What about your wife and kids," I asked.

His white teeth flashed in the starlight. "I am without the dubious advantages of a family. None would mourn if I should come back without my head."

The hole was a hole only at first glance. On closer examination it proved to be the entrance to a cavern of such vastness that we were staggered by the immensity of it. The smaller temples and buildings were light enough to rest safely on the sixty to eighty feet thickness of limestone, but not the *Castillo*. When at last we had wound down and stood thunderstruck at what we were seeing, Phil flashed his powerful beam and then we could appreciate the whole. The *Castillo* was bigger in its entirety than Cheops. The mightiest pyramid I had ever seen stood revealed before us. We knew then that what we could see of the *Castillo* was not merely a large pyramid with a temple on top but one that had begun on the floor of the cave and built right on through the thick crust of limestone that formed the roof; what we had seen of it was less than a third of the total size. Its sides glittered with untold centuries of dripstone as the lights struck it and, with the millions of stalactitic reflections, the whole place seemed alive with moving, crawling light.

José muttered something under his breath and crossed himself. Pepe sucked in a harsh lungful of air and Soldarez's teeth clicked shut audibly. After we had partially recovered from the impact of the scene we began a careful search of the floorlike surface of the cave. It was damp but there were signs of human habitation or occupation. Tracks, hundreds of them led off in what I took to be the direction of the *cenote*. We examined the pyramid first just to let its fabulous immensity creep into our minds.

"How the hell did they keep water from washing in around that structure?" I said, while the question was repeated back and forth in echo until at last it shuddered away in the distance and died.

I broke out with cold sweat while Phil made a shushing gesture at me and pointed to the roof where the structure poked through. "Notice that stone and mortar work?" he whispered.

I nodded, trying to keep my hide from crawling off my back at the sighing echoes of his whisper as it plumbed the last crack in the cave. "There is some seepage, of course, but no real flow of water." This time he tried speaking low but the result was even worse. The echo scraped about in cracks and crannies like a runaway bass viol and finally hummed itself to death in the distance.

After fighting off the effects of the titanic immensity of this part of the *Castillo,* we followed tracks and came to the *cenote.* We walked out on a smooth stone slab four feet above water level and looked into the green depths of this place of mystery. Did they really toss maidens into its depths to mollify Yum Chaac, the rain god and god of a good many other important functions? Had Edward H. Thompson really cleaned it when he dredged it or were there millenniums of accumulation still buried beneath the rocks that sometimes crumbled from the scarred sides?

We stood there silently, wondering and thinking. Phil sprayed the light around casually and then said, "I wonder why this entrance wasn't found when Thompson had divers in here."

"Probably," suggested José reasonably, "because he wasn't looking for entrances but things at the bottom of the *cenote*. Note, too, that this place is nearly obscured by bushes."

"Probably," said Phil shortly. He was not accustomed to having people hit him in the face with obviosities. I got tickled and had to muffle a laugh.

Phil turned around and said, "Let's examine the walls around this area. Maybe we'll find rooms."

We examined until I was fagged and sweating in spite of the damp chilliness of the place. We didn't find any rooms but we found places where they might have been, the doors stopped up with the usual Mayan white cement and stone long turned green and black with mold. They were glazed with dripstone and weren't new by any means.

"The good doctor Moffett will go wild when he hears about this," I mumbled and was surprised to hear nothing in the way of an echo. The acoustics of this place were uncanny.

"I'm hoping the good doctor will not hear of it," said Phil, ill-temperedly. "He is entirely too harmless and affable. He's not as hot on Mayan lore as he pretends. He's full of legend and that's about all."

I let go a yell to further test the acoustic effect of hearing my voice fall like a dead cat on a thick carpet. But there also seemed to be a musical note that started and stopped suddenly. I opened my mouth and really let go; not long afterward I wished I hadn't. The thin keen musical note was heard again but it gathered volume until it sounded like a million mad violins, like a cloud of banshees whirled about in a titanic whirlwind. José staggered against me and went to his knees and Phil put his hands to his ears and leaned against the rugged wall. Finally, as though someone had cut off a switch, it ceased. For three seconds there was a silence equally as harrowing as the sound had been; then about three hundred tons of stalactite burst loose from the roof and fell with a crash, showering us with stone splinters. The resulting echoes magnified a million times just simply beat us flat. For fifteen minutes, maybe less, we just lay there frazzled and knocked out.

Phil sat up and shook chips of dripstone from him. "The next time you pull a stunt like that," he said carefully, "I shall take it as a personal affront and proceed to beat your brains out with the nearest handy cudgel."

José, still my friend, chuckled softly. "He could hardly be expected to forsee such an occurrence, Captain."

"He'd better turn crystal-gazer, then," snarled Phil, getting up. His man got up also with a bitter glance at me and began to clean the debris from his beloved Winchester. We started walking again. Around a corner in the corridor we entered into a fairyland. It looked like a gigantic ballroom with crystal pillars, except that it was endless; it seemed to go on forever.

"This is all for now," said Phil with finality. "We'd be lost as soon as we lost sight of the Castle." He swept the place again with his light; the reflections were echoed like sounds and the place lit up all over as though indirectly illuminated.

Phil cut off the flash and we stood there holding our breath when, from some place else, it lit up again briefly then flickered gradually out.

"Ah," breathed Phil, "there are others inside."

"Maybe a watch should be kept at the entrance," said José hopefully.

"Oh, why try?" said Phil bitterly. "Must be ten other entrances. Ches, I didn't think I could become so discouraged. We've nothing to work on. Our opposition remains in the dark and shoots at us—"

As a prophet, Phil was a killer. There was a sharp *snaaak* of a high-powered bullet and José gasped and fell backward. Phil's light swept toward the area where the flash came from but he had enough sense to hold it at arm's length. It was promptly shot from his hand. This time Pepé unlimbered his Winchester and the place began to rock and roll from the stunning explosions, not having yet recovered from those aimed at us.

José struggled to his feet again and handed me his flashlight. "I'm … I might … drop it, Señor."

"That did it," snarled Phil, starting forward. "You stay with José, Ches. Come on, Pepé."

José had taken one clean through the left shoulder and in falling had cut the hell out of his leg with his machete. He was bleeding pretty badly. I picked him up—he didn't weigh over a hundred and five pounds—and walked to where Phil and Pepé were looking at a man sprawled on his face atop his rifle. Pepé had gotten him twice out of five shots, firing in the dark at a flash. I was suddenly glad he was on our side. It was getting closer and closer. We had been missed some but now one of us had gotten it. A little closer and José would have guided his last tourist.

Phil stood up, his eyes boiling and his face as hard as the feet of the *Castillo*. "Maybe this is the way we'll have to do it, Ches. Kill them all. We're on the way all right. This is one of them."

"How do you know?"

He handed me the rifle.

It was a Mauser that must have cost close to a thousand bucks. It was a beautiful weapon with the very finest engraving on the barrel and foregrip, a Zeiss scope that itself was worth a small sporting fortune and the receiver and stock were almost hidden with gold, silver and ivory inlay.

José loosed a groan that reminded me of his wounds. "We've got to get him out," I said. "Quick."

We got him out quick, gathered our watchers and made tracks to the Mayaland Lodge where we rooted Dr. Moffett out of his bed and watched him sew up the nasty slash in José's leg and bandage the wound in his shoulder. "Hospital," he said succinctly as he stood up. Phil nodded and went away. He disinterred Señor Barbachano from a deep sleep and together they arranged for a car which sped José and me back to Merida. This time the driver was a guide, name of Felipe, a little brown man with soft steady brown eyes and total disregard for the potential dangers of which we warned him before we left. He had merely shrugged, smiled and climbed into his blue Chrysler.

We left José in good hands. Felipe and I started back toward Chichen in a fog thick enough to cut up and put in your pocket.

"I've seen fish swimming in water thinner than this," complained Felipe as he grazed a cow who was standing in the middle of the road, contentedly chewing away at something that seemed tasty to her.

I didn't like the fog for a number of reasons, few of which had anything to do with cows and cars. At the speed we were crawling along nothing could happen except a skinned cow or a bent fender. Too many people knew we had gone to Merida and almost any place they could be lying in wait with a Gatling gun or a satchel charge.

As a prophet, I was no small change myself; some ten miles from Chichen it happened about as normally as anything could. A boulder had tumbled from a steep shoulder and effectively blocked the road. Felipe said something unnice in Spanish, stopped the car and got out to see if the place was made for a detour. "It happens occasionally, señor," he said as I came up with my own gun out. That was smart but walking directly into the glare of the headlights wasn't. I knew it when a raucous voice rang out in my ear. "Drop the gun, Markham, or I'll blow you all over the macadam."

I dropped it while Felipe stood casually by, not seeming to be particularly interested.

CHAPTER ELEVEN

TWO OF THEM came out of the murk. One of them was a tall lithe Englishman, apparently the one who had spoken. The other looked as squarehead as scrapple, with stiff blond hair in a crewcut, thick neck and a body that was heavy but as hard as muscle gets. You could tell it.

"Good afternoon, honorable Bertie," I said affably as the Kraut picked up my .45, "and to you also, Fritz. When did you get off the submarine?" Me and my big mouth. They went as stiff as corpses for a moment; then the Limey clouted me on the side of the head with his Browning—negligently, sort of, although it didn't feel that way. "You talk too much, Yank," he said suavely, "and you know too much. Moreover, you're lucky as well as that Spig, Soldarez. You're too lucky or too good for the sort of peasantry we usually leave such chores to. May I confidently predict the end of the line?"

"You already have," I said. "Where? Here?"

"Oh, no. That would be unwise and, as a matter of fact, we would like to know what you know. I suspect you know too much. Oh, Loder, will you frisk the brown dwarf?"

"I am a guide, señor," said Felipe, whose eyes were now hard; he didn't like being called a dwarf, "and therefore unarmed."

"Oh, quite, quite. Nevertheless, we shall see."

Loder was apparently contemptuous of Felipe and gave him a few pats and stood back.

"Now," said our amusing friend, "on the other side of the rock is another conveyance. You will proceed thereto."

We proceeded thereto and were thrown into the back of a tattery two-door sedan. They climbed in front with Loder behind the wheel and Bertie pointing his Browning automatic impartially between us.

"There are no handles on the window lifts," he said, "so I'd advise that you remain quiet and do not force me to needlessly inconvenience you—as with a painful pill in the pylorus."

We rode along for several miles until I expected to see Chichen loom out of the mist momentarily, then we made a left turn and plunged into the jungle. The road was fair, having been cut through the tangle years ago, but jungle had reclaimed a good bit of it and reached out at the car continually with branches and vines.

"May I smoke?" asked Felipe with such seriousness that honorable Bertie laughed.

"Go ahead, little man. I would not deprive you of that last pleasure. Unfortunately, you probably know nothing and therefore are of no use to us."

Felipe took out a cigarette and placed it between his lips, then began a struggle with apparently damp matches. After cursing them softly in Spanish for a moment he managed to strike a light after using several of them. There was a brilliant flash for a second then abrupt darkness as he dropped them. The next thing was a cracking explosion and Bertie, still sitting sideways, slid off the seat onto the floor.

"I should enjoy shooting you in the back of the head," said Felipe, hissing like a rattler ready to strike. "However, if you will be so kind as to turn this vehicle around …"

Lober, as stolid as an ox, stopped the car and instantly it seemed we were surrounded.

"Name of a little white goat!" barked Felipe savagely and fired straight into the face of a man who had thrust his arm in at the window.

Loder came over the back seat at me like a diving tackler and from there on I was busy. He had me pinned down where I couldn't do any good and he was beating wildly at my head with a short metal bolt. Felipe was crowded so badly that he was nearly squeezed to death and he couldn't use his gun. In the melee he was dragged bodily from the car.

Thus given a little room I managed to claw my way to a spot on Loder where a man can stand to take no punishment and I clamped down as hard as I could. Loder let out a bawl like a wounded steer, dropping his bolt and falling backward in a frenzied effort to escape. On the floor I located a rusty jack and slammed him squarely in the mouth, feeling the low frequency grate of breaking teeth. Then I was dragged from the car by a guy who didn't know I had the jack. I doubt that he ever realized it because as soon as I got room I swung it full-armed and it squashed into his head as though it had been an overripe watermelon. Hot debris spattered over me and then I noticed that I was standing alone. There were no more men. I used my flash and located Felipe in death grips with a man twice his size, but my chauffeur was not a guy who counted his small stature as any particular deficiency in battle.

He had simply carved the guy to ribbons. The man's clothes were in ragged sliced tatters and his butchered flesh stood up in ugly uneven lumps. Blood still gushed from a severed carotid artery in ghastly spurts. Someone had tapped Felipe on the back of the head but he had made a last despairing stab and buried the knife to the hilt in the man's belly; he still held onto it. I dragged him off to get him away from that fountain of gore and as I did he sat up.

"Did we emerge victorious?" he asked.

"We emerged," I said, "but we'd better get out of here before some more men get wind of us. We weren't exactly quiet, you know. I'll drive because you must not feel—"

He chuckled. "I am a man of peace but I find myself strangely stimulated by this act of war. Driving is what I'm paid to do." With that, dripping with another man's blood and still groggy, he jumped into the driver's seat, turned the car around and we spun merrily back toward the Mayaland without further incident.

Dawn shone pink through the mist as we approached the last curve that would take us down the incline to the Lodge. The *Castillo* loomed wet-black and awesome as we passed, its temple momentarily obscured by the mist. In the background I could see the tails of the twin serpents atop the Temple of the Warriors.

It was too early for tourists to be stirring so we managed to get lost without causing any screaming and fainting. We were sights that would cause a strong man to seek the hospital. Felipe was a mass of darkening scarlet and I was spattered with gore.

One look at me and Phil's hands knotted up. "Not again."

"Yeah. I'll tell you about it when I've had a bath. Right now I'm just before flipping my cookies."

I bathed and lit a cigarette, puffing at it hungrily. I hadn't thought about smoking before.

I sat on the bed in my nothings. "They rolled a boulder into the road and blocked it. We thought it was a natural occurrence and got out to see if we could get around it. We were sitting ducks in the headlights."

"Doubtless," he commented dryly. "Then what?"

"They bundled us into a car on the other side of the rocks and after a while turned off to the left on a side road. Felipe had a gun secreted on his person some place where Loder ... Oh—we have a live one, by the way. Tied up hand and foot in the car we took. Loder missed the gun somehow so after this Limey got careless Felipe just ups with it and blasts him right in the kisser. Felipe and I had some fun with the others who happened to be around. The Limey and Loder are out there but the Limey is dead as a salted sprat."

Phil sighed and got up. "We ought to take a look at that road."

We did, but we might have saved ourselves the trouble. It ran down to a clearing where some Indian had had a corn patch. Another decrepit car was there but nothing else. The old corn stalks were beaten down in a wide area.

Phil whipped himself on a lean leg with a piece of cornstalk and muttered in Spanish. "Let's go," he bit out finally. "I thought this would be a dry run." It had been dry because even the bodies we left had been removed. We were pretty silent going back, Phil because he was thinking and me because I expected a hunk of lead between the horns just about any time from behind any bush. I thought about Verna and could see her stretching her gorgeous body between the sheets, probably with nothing on and the soft white stuff caressing her in intimate spots and riding the swells of her breasts.

I could see the finely turned perfection of her ankles and see the poignance of her face which showed in unguarded moments that her blithe act was not untouched with unhappiness.

"I'm glad we have Loder," said Phil unexpectedly.

"Well, I am too, since you are. Why?"

"I'm going to try an experiment."

"Like what?"

"In fact, I'm going to try two experiments. One will involve Dr. Moffett and the other will just involve you and me."

"What will they be?"

"In good time," he said, irritatingly. "I expected to get a good bite when we went into the cave but we didn't. The men said no one entered the same place we did."

"You opined once that there might be ten other places."

"I still think so. Anyhow, the man who shot José might have already been in there. We weren't exactly quiet, you know."

"About that—I've been meaning to ask. What the hell made that god-awful noise when I yelled?"

He shrugged. "This seems to be a place of queer sounds. I've been thinking about that. Remember that long thin stalactite that nearly reached the floor?"

"Yes."

"Well, that was the one that fell. I've decided that your yell and a combination of echoes must have set up some sort of self-energizing vibration and the thing just vibrated itself to pieces, making that keen note."

"It was keen enough to shave with," I said with a shudder.

Back at the Lodge we had a big breakfast and sat a while smoking. Verna came down looking fresh and edible, dressed in white shirt and blue slacks. "Good morning," she said brightly.

We grunted good mornings, which made her look at me sharply. "What's wrong, Ches?"

"Nothing that I can tell you about, kid. I didn't get any sleep and I'm a bear."

Her face fell a little and she shivered. "Ches, I'm getting scared."

"Why don't you go back to Merida?"

"Oh, hush. You couldn't drive me back. I'm sorry, I won't ask you any more questions."

She didn't but Dr. Moffett did, not that he got anything that sounded like a answer. Then Phil threw his bombshell. "Dr. Moffett, we have a prisoner and I'd like your cooperation in treating him."

"Treating him, Captain? Is he injured?"

"He's injured," I said. "I caved the front of his face in with a tire jack."

"That's not what I mean," said Phil. "He'll have to be treated, all right. His injuries are painful and disfiguring but not serious. I'd like to question him under narco-synthesis."

The little man seemed to grow taut and his little eyes darted hither and thither. "Er ... well, there is naturally a question of ethics involved, but if it is a formal and legal request I'll—"

"I'm making the request," said Soldarez, a trifle hard. "My position is legal enough although I should not like to be put through a lot of red tape in order to accomplish my purpose."

"Very well. After breakfast. I shall have to read up on the technique. Might take a little while to find it in my books. Say, nine o'clock?"

"That should suffice. However, I'd like for you to look at the prisoner as soon as you eat. I think he is in considerable pain."

The doctor examined Loder after breakfast and gave him a shot, saying that the big job would be one for a dentist and not for an M.D.; then he left to read up. So we thought.

At ten Phil sent a boy to see about the doctor. Ten minutes later the boy came back and said the little man was nowhere to be found. Phil snorted and cursed heartily. "There goes one part of my experiment. I didn't expect him to disappear. He can't have gone far."

"Unless he went into the cave," I said. "In which case he wouldn't have to go far to be far gone."

Phil summoned Pepé and was put out to find that half the group of Mayans had gone into the cave to bring out the body of the man Pepe dropped the night before.

"Who ordered them in?" snarled Phil.

"*El señor doctor,*" said Pepé stolidly. "He brings a message from you about nine o'clock saying to go beneath the earth and bring up the body. I detailed men to obey orders."

"All right. It couldn't be helped, I suppose, and it does cinch one thing."

"What?" I asked, interested in what it cinched.

"The doctor is mixed up in it somewhere. He wasn't supposed to know that we had left a body in there. Chances are the men won't find it. He ran when faced with having to dope one of his own men. Pepé, take what men are left and turn over every rock in Chichen until you find him."

He was right on all counts, it seemed. The doctor had been swallowed and the most dilligent search couldn't turn up a trace of him.

We flopped around the Lodge, dispirited and low with Verna doing her best, but it was hardly enough to raise our glooms. Phil, who had been puffing on a cigarette, snapped to and got up. "I'd forgotten my other experiment. Come on, Ches. Verna, you may come if you wish." She bounded to her feet and followed us out to where one of the Mayans stood guard over the car that still held Loder.

"*Achtung!*" barked Phil and like my German friend in Maryland he nearly bumped his head snapping straight. His face was a mess, his lips cut and shredded and the whole front from chin to eyes a puffed ugly mess.

"Get out of the car," ordered Phil in good German.

"I spigging Anglish," mumbled the man. Phil made the Mayan tie a tight blindfold on Loder so he couldn't see a thing.

"Not as well as I speak German," said Phil and we started for the Ball Court.

The closer we came the more nervous Loder got until at last when we seated him on the stone execution chair he burst out. "I haff did noddings. Vhat iss you doing to me ... vhat ..."

"Shut up," said Phil and cuffed him painlessly on a thick shoulder. We tied him carefully to the stone knobs and with a gesture Phil ordered the Mayan to take away the blindfold.

The minute Loder saw where he was he squealed like a branded steer and, with a single herculean wrench, tore away the cords that bound him and took off like a scared quail.

The Mayan threw his rifle to his shoulder and before Phil could yell at him not to shoot, cut Loder down with one slug. He hadn't gotten twenty yards.

Phil was mouthing Hispanic curses under his breath until he discovered that Loder only had a bullet through the fleshy part of his left thigh.

He rolled the groaning man over and shook him. "Why did you run?"

The man's face was drenched with the sweat of horror. His eyes rolled and his breath came in short jerks. "Dot blace ... I am seeing a man killed dere."

"Who was he?"

"Hiss name vass Blovitch. He vass Rossian."

"Sounds like a Commie version of Joe Blow," I said.

"What had he done?" asked Phil.

The German shrugged. "I vas nod knowing."

"Do they kill men for failure?"

"Times are dot dey do."

"And who are 'they?' " asked Verna, coming into the conversation.

Loder shut his jaws tight and winced at the pain of his shattered teeth. "Nod knowing."

"I think you do," said Phil silkily.

Loder only looked sullen and shook his head.

"All right." Phil gestured to the Mayan and in less than three minutes Loder was trussed to the executioner's seat. This time he wouldn't break away. The Mayan, distrusting our cotton twine, had substituted henequin and it was strong enough to hang him.

"You have one more chance to talk Loder. *Der Vaterland* is beaten and any such gang as you're now running with will be also hunted down. Tell us what you know."

Sweat streaked his face and a groan of mortal anguish ripped from his very depths.

Phil tossed a stone accurately and the Ball Court was filled with the silent power of high frequency sound waves thumming in our vitals. "Time is growing short, Loder."

"Cudt me away from dis blace." His head sank on his chest. "I tell you vhat I could."

It was a nice story, a story that sent Phil and me into a fever of activity. Radiograms in supersecret code flashed to capitals all over the world—that is, Washington got hers first and sent the rest.

From the interior of Mexico came a flight of lend-lease F-47s that landed at the Merida field, disgorging lean leathery pilots all of whom embraced Phil and he them.

"The sub is based at Cabo Blanco," said Phil, after the meeting was completed to the last back slap. "Does that show on your maps?"

It didn't, but one pilot thought he could find it. "That won't do," Phil pointed out. "Military planes over that area after they know we have Loder will be too suspicious. If Lieutenant Ramirez will allow me to take his plane I'll lead the rest in. I know where it is. I ordered five-hundred-pound demolition bombs."

"That's what we have," said Captain Reyes, the leader of the squadron. "We also have full chests of fifty caliber armor-piercing ammo."

"We might need it. I hope you understand, Ramirez."

Lieutenant Ramirez, a slim light-skinned son of Cortez, bowed and smiled. "Sir, you are one of the reasons I'm now flying. I would like to go but I can see the need of staying. Please do not consider my feelings in this matter."

Again we were to be disappointed. They combed the area for days but not a trace of the sub did they see. They heard of her, though. A small freighter of the Pan American Fruit Line carrying twenty accommodation passengers was sent to the bottom by surface shellfire with all except five hands. All passengers died. The sub then closed in and handed the few survivors an ultimatum to deliver to the Mexican and United States governments. It stated in effect that a wave of indiscriminate sinkings would begin, without regard to loss of life and no warnings given, unless all efforts to apprehend this group that called itself "The Reckoners" were immediately stopped.

Phil gave an outraged grunt when it was belatedly delivered to him and immediately wired Washington. Ship companies were promptly ordered to steer their vessels wide of the Gulf of Mexico or, better still, to berth them. They naturally set up a yowl that resounded heavenward. They demanded destroyer escorts and I don't know what all. The destroyers were sent, however, as well as a carrier and the Gulf became churned with propellers of many sizes.

Another ship, a fast new liner out of Santos, was sent to the bottom just before dawn one day, but nearly all the passengers and crew were saved. Papers began to speak in ugly tones and uglier hints and Naval officers gathered a few more grey hairs than the expected complement.

Phil and I worked ourselves to the nub, explored the cave and the entire area around Chichen trying to discover more entrances. We blazed a trail with black paint into the depths of the cave until we must have gone ten miles from the ruins. When we saw no signs of habitation and no sign of an end to the cavern, we retraced our steps.

Norcross arrived by plane from Africa and immediately disappeared into the jungle near Cabo Blanco.

"Think he's lost?" I asked Phil one night after dinner.

"Him?" He chuckled. "He's Bre'r Rabbit in the briar patch. You couldn't lose him in *Grande Chaco*."

"Why didn't he stick around for briefing?"

"He did. I spoke with him for ten minutes. He has a theory about where these ships are hiding."

"If his theory is as good as their hiding place, we can just sit back and watch."

Phil's face grew hard. "If Norcross comes in here and breaks this thing right under our noses we'll never live it down."

"I'll do all right," I said easily. "I have no reputation like you do. Anyhow, you—I mean *we* white card men are supposed to work all for one and one for all."

Phil flushed. "I gave him every scrap of information we have."

"I'm kidding. Did he suggest what his theory might look like?"

Phil looked downcast. "He did and I must say he certainly hit on a hot point the first thing. He thinks that cave has an opening to the sea, maybe a tremendous subterranean gulf that the sub can enter at any time and the other craft at low tide. He thinks the cave can and has been traversed from here to that area."

"He didn't go through the cave, did he?"

"No. His idea was to follow the coast line on foot until he finds the place. Actually, although it's a shuddering thought, I doubt that it can be found in any other way."

"So we sit here and let Norcross lacerate our pride?"

He shrugged. "What can we do?"

I got up. I felt like a fool or Napoleon—maybe more like Napoleon. "Let's get outfitted, take two burros, pack them and follow the cave. Take a compass bearing on Cabo Blanco and work eventually in that direction no matter where the cave takes us."

Phil looked at me like I was nuts for a moment, then smacked his hands together. "It's a thought. Maybe we'll find something. Maybe we'll run into a chasm that'll turn us back. At the outside maybe we can get through and find the place."

"Who'll we take?"

"Pepé and three Mayans. That'll be enough because we don't know how long we'll be in there. I'll see Pepé and tell him to make preparations."

"I'll see Verna and tell her I'm going on a trip."

"If you must, but there must be no mention of what the trip is."

I met her coming in the front entrance clad in dazzling white shorts and a scarlet silk shirt. My heart went into my mouth for a moment, not so much from the spectacle she presented but the fact that this might be my last time to see her. I'd talked myself into a spot I couldn't duck. Whirling her behind a hibiscus bush I kissed her like it was to last a lifetime.

"Golly ... Ches ... Any more of those left?"

"Don't joke," I said severely. "I'm going to leave. I'll be back but I don't know when."

"Something break?"

"No, this is an effort to make something break. We don't know what'll come of it, if anything."

Her eyes grew damp and her lips trembled. "I'm sorry I said what I did about your kiss. Oh, Ches, you felt like it might be the last, didn't you?"

I squirmed. It had impressed me that maybe it was the last one but I didn't want her to know it.

"Shucks," I said hollowly. "Nothing to it. We'll be back before you know it."

Her face was straight and serious, her eyes bottomless like the *cenote*. She came close and overpowered me with the clean fragrance of her hair and body. "When do you leave?"

"In the morning."

"May I have part of tonight?"

My throat choked up and I nodded, unable to speak. She turned with a flash of smooth legs and was gone.

Fernando, Junior came in then and caught me by the arm. "We've been neglecting each other," he said affably. "What about a gill or two in the bar?"

"That's the first sensible thing I've heard this evening," I said, remembering something I heard a guy name of Markham suggest ten minutes previously.

"My father tells me you and Captain Soldarez are up to your necks in something hot."

I nodded and tasted the 1902 Yucatean brandy to which I had become immensely partial. "That's right. Sorry we can't tell you more."

His white teeth flashed in a smile. "I wasn't trying to pick you. You two have found more big stuff in a few days than archeologists have turned up in years."

I nodded. "You'll be able to really play up the *Castillo* when you get that cave wired for lights. It's a fairyland down there. It makes me shudder to hear the echoes the way that cave swallows them up after a time."

He nodded and lit a cigarette. "Everything new is something else to put on the travel folder. We should give you two a free trip to Uxmal. There's no telling what you'd find."

"You'd better explore the possibility that the Mayans used this cave as a means of travel, maybe even to Uxmal. It appears to be endless."

"We'll do that. Oh, Miss Martell. Won't you have a drink?"

"I'll have several if I may," she said, dimpling deliciously and looking very lovely and virginal in a dress of some pure white material that clung softly to her lush curves.

"By the way, Fernando," I said after Verna had been served, "is the jeep in use tonight?"

"I don't think so. We generally use it to get to the more inaccessible spots. You want it?"

"I'd like to borrow it for a ride, if I may."

"See Roberto. He'll be able to tell you. No, I must find my father now, anyway. I'll see to it myself."

He bowed to us and went out, leaving behind him a strange aura of old Spain and twentieth century, something I had also noticed in his father.

Verna moved a warm thigh against mine and held it there while bolts of eager demand leaped into being from the contact.

"Hear it, Ches?"

"I heard it," I said huskily. "It's music older than these ruins but always as new as a water lily." Her eyes softened and a hand crept over mine to rest there quietly. "I didn't know you could say such sweet things."

"This is Yucatan," I said, still feeling poetic, "where one's best is always better, where stars are bigger and the moon is brighter. The favorable rate of exchange works all around."

"I want to get lost in the starlight," she said softly, "and see how far the rate of exchange does go."

"Let me see Phil," I said, getting up. "Meet me at the entrance."

Phil and Pepé had their heads together as I came up. "Do you suppose I may keep a date?" I asked.

He nodded. "Just don't make it last too long. You'll need sleep tomorrow when you can't get it."

"We won't be long," I promised.

CHAPTER TWELVE

THE RATE of exchange was certainly at work that night. We had found a little knoll off the main road. The sky overhead was an intense dark blue vault spangled by trillions of stars, making a light that was shadowless and as soft as mist. In its illumination Verna was a naiad of such stupendous attraction that I felt a little giddy as we looked into each other's eyes, silently and with an understanding that transcended speech or gesture.

Her hands touched my face and I could feel them tremble as she fought the dynamic urge to fling her body into the activity it demanded so urgently. Slowly and with the tight rein of discipline strongly held we touched and tasted almost detachedly the stinging electric presence of the other.

Nature approved of us because there was a sweet breeze blowing across us laden with the fragrance of frangipani and the expected mosquitoes were not present. Far across the jungle a jaguar coughed cautiously and a spider monkey screamed as though the big cat were breathing down its neck.

Night birds chuckled softly back and forth and something screamed long and sobbingly, making us draw closer together.

"This can't be the last time, Ches," she whispered.

"It won't be," I assured her, lacking assurance myself. I drew her close, letting the fragrant heat of her body set my own blood afire.

"It can't be," she repeated. "Nothing this perfect can die. Not now, anyhow. Soon my clothes will open and my breasts will peek forth and you'll kiss them, making me faint and dizzy, wanting you until I ache and burn with wanting. Your hands will creep over me and into forbidden places and I'll come closer to fainting. You'll take me then and beat me weak with joy. You will bruise my skin and flesh then your caresses will magically heal in the same manner that they bruised.

"Lightning will blast us loose from everything of reality and we will float in a fog of delicious nothingness." She sighed as her lips closed over mine.

We broke, breathlessly listening to the echoes of the thunders that the touch of our lips had set into being. I reached in the back seat and threw a rough woolen blanket out on the grassy ground, then stepped out. She stood in the seat nearest me, ready to be taken down, but I couldn't resist the darkening trails of marvelous thighs that reached upward into the dusky cavern of her skirt. I slid my palms up their smooth hot surfaces until I realized that they had passed her hips and were encircling her waist ... no obstacles. I lifted her close and let her slide downward feeling the thin material of the dress skin upward leaving her as she descended. I held her and tasted the warmth of her body as it pressed close to me; I kissed her, thoroughly reeling to the vivid sweetness of her darting tongue then I released her and spread the blanket.

"There may be *garrapatos*," I said.

"What are they?" she asked languidly as she stretched on the blanket. "Snakes?"

"No, ticks."

She sighed and stretched with such wanton seductiveness that I felt a swift chill strike me. "In that event, damn the torpedoes or the *garrapatos*—and if it didn't sound so bitchy I'd finish the quotation."

I leaned over to kiss her and noticed that her dress had come open in some manner and the full hemispheres of her breasts, taut from passion and cool from the night breeze, erect and trembling from the deep thrashing emotion that activated them, were eagerly awaiting my lips. As I touched them her hands pressed against my ears moving my head to her own desires, her body wrenching free of all discipline now and seeking its own.

Under the stars of Yucatan, in the cool breezes that caressed them like feathery fingers, a man and a woman went straight to heaven. That they had to return was a matter for great rejoicing, for there would be other such journeys, each more wonderful than the next ... and her cry of unendurable ecstasy was answered by the cry of an animal in the distance ... then the purple night closed over us like a blanket and the body that had given so much joy now gave comfort and warmth.

The stairway leading from behind the west wall of the Ball Court down into the cavern was wider and more adaptable to four-footed navigation than most of the Mayan stairways; they generally make two-footed travel a matter of chance and possible contusions. So we managed to make the burros take the plunge but not without considerable coaxing and much corporal punishment. But we made it. Pepé carried the brush and paint bucket which would take up trail blazing after we had gone the distance that we had previously gone. There were plenty of flashlight batteries and one flood light which we used for traveling.

There was little or no talking as the daubs of black paint were clearly visible and the floor was relatively easy traveling. Occasionally a rifle would scrape against a pipe of dripstone, making the cave hideous with battering echoes that made my hair stand up. The burros, being creatures of nature, greeted this phenomenon without turning a hair and threatened to bolt only when one of them brayed out some protest in burro language and very nearly made both of them jump out of their skin. The sound, magnified, was burro-like, all right, but like no burro either of them had ever heard before. It took the combined strength of all of us to keep the tiny animals from taking off, packs and all, which would have placed us in a very pretty predicament, indeed.

Exactly four hours after entering the cave of crystal we came to the end of the black paint and Pepe had to go to work.

Six hours later and God knows how deep in the bowels of the earth, men and beasts were fagged. All, that is, except Phil. If he was tired he was keeping it a secret and went around in a big circle, snooping. He came back balancing on the uneven water-worn rocks like a ballet dancer.

"Success," he said holding up a cigarette butt.

"What is it?"

"Lucky. They're smoked all over and someone not accustomed to Mexican cigarettes would pick an American brand if it was available."

I nodded and watched Pepé set up a fire in a can—alcohol poured over sand and set ablaze. He was going to make tea and tea I wanted right then because the damp chill of the cave had begun to work through and gnaw at my bones. I watched him pour the water.

Water … *water* … *waterworn* … How in the hell could rocks be waterworn in here?

I got up, as bushed as I was, and did some snooping of my own. I picked up a handful of round smooth stones and approached Phil, who had found what he sought—signs of man—and was resting.

"Gold nuggets?" he asked brightly.

"No. Waterworn rocks. Figure that one out."

He picked up a rock and looked it over, flashed his light on it and tasted it. He was just one step ahead of the biggest burro who was now industriously licking a round smooth boulder.

"Salt," he croaked.

"Salt," I peeped.

"Whonk," sang the burro happily, and all of us were busy for five minutes coaxing echo-itis out of the two beasts.

Phil and I panted and looked at each other. "The tide comes up in here," he said hollowly.

"Can you swim?" I asked crazily.

"I can but damned if I want to. Okay, Pepé, douse your fire. We must hunt high ground."

We found suitable high ground in something under an hour and luckily it was one of those places where noises fell dead and we weren't constantly harried by echoes.

"Whonk," said a tired burro, then stiffened and prepared to bolt, in effect, covering his ears with his hooves. Nothing happened so he heaved a sigh of relief and promptly sat down, making us lift him bodily to get the pack off.

I don't know where Phil unearthed C-rations but if they were lend lease they were now a ripe old age and should be rather spicy. They were edible, which for C-rations is saying a lot but we were tired and hungry.

Pepé spread a thin ugly-looking gadget on a smooth place, making me wonder who had ever considered it fit for a human body to sleep on; but when he located a tube and began to puff into it I understood and couldn't wait until he was through to try it. I fell dead instantly and felt like pushing Phil off into the water when he woke me ... Water? Sure enough. We were on an island now and as far as we could see was water at least six feet deep without a ripple or a sign of current. I dipped my finger and tasted. Not briny but salty, as though a lot of salt water had mixed with a lot of fresh water.

"Now what?" I asked.

"By the time we've eaten I think it will have fallen," he said. "It's going down pretty swiftly."

"Nuts," I scoffed. "There isn't a ripple in it."

"I noticed that and it made me wonder. There is a solution."

"I'm sure glad of that," I said with bluff heartiness. "Give."

"Well, between us and the sea is a low hanging wall. The water comes through the opening and rises above the point of entry. When the tide goes out, until the level is equal to that of the opening there isn't any surface disturbance."

I grunted. "It's an explanation, all right. However, a thought occurs to me."

"I was afraid of that," he said cattily. "What now?"

"With all these echoes and stuff, why don't we send them a note by Pepé telling them we're coming?"

He nodded slowly, a frown cutting the marble smoothness of his almost too perfect brow. "That thought has been plaguing me for some time, but ..."

"Just a moment. About how far would you say we are from the coast?"

He looked at me enigmatically. "Do you expect to cave it all the way to the coast?"

I shrugged. "Well, I will admit that Norcross' way looks better the further we get in here. But wasn't that your idea?"

He shook his head. "Not exactly. I think the opening, the sea entry is well-hidden, maybe by overhanging jungle, and probably very narrow. Just the same I expect it to extend inland quite some distance. In fact, I don't think we're more than twenty-five miles in the cave, if that much. True, we've been traveling approximately two miles an hour, the reason having been just explained, but that would put us approximately twenty miles from *el Castillo*. We haven't been traveling airline, either."

"I'm not ordinarily this thick," I explained, "but just what explains our rate of progress?"

"Tide water. Through the years it has made floors in this place except in spots. If you were ever in any of the big caves in the United States you must realize that this one is practically a freeway."

He was right. I had been in a couple and after you left the tourist limits you took life, limb and shins in your hands. We had been traveling practically on a level and with very little difficulty.

"Have you gotten as far as estimating how far this inland gulf might extend?"

He shook his head. "Not yet, but I'm hoping it will be quite far."

"You got any boats?" I asked, sarcastically.

"Oh, yes. A three-man inflatable raft on the burro. And a tire pump."

I gave him a glance of sheer admiration. "What else have you bought that doesn't show on the surface?"

"One M-1928 Thompson sub-machine gun with six loaded drums of ammo. Ah, there's your ripple." While we were talking the water had been receding swiftly and now as though a long fish were making a wave, you could see the surface striated toward the flow of water.

"About noise," Phil went on. "I've decided to send Pepé ahead to scout. He's a scout you'll be proud of. He'll range far ahead of us and report back only when he has something to report."

"What about his light?"

"The reflections aren't as great here and I think by the time he reaches a danger area they'll be gone. The action of salt water will have taken most of the gloss from the dripstone."

I wanted to ask him what he expected to find but I didn't dare because he had never been there and it would been like asking him about Santa Claus.

After the water receded we made our way into a gloom like midnight in the middle of an iceberg except that it wasn't that cold.

Pepé forged ahead of us, still trail-blazing, and by the time we stopped for chow we couldn't see a sign of his light.

"As I said," Phil began, "the gloss is getting less and so is the reflection. We'd better keep our eyes peeled for high spots since we're walking right on the bottom of the river, so to speak."

From then on travel was a succession of nightmares, of neck-breaking races to high places to avoid sudden flash floods of tide-water. Twice we had to hold tight around a corner until the water got high, then swim for some slippery pyramidal rise in the cavern floor. During those times we practically had to carry the burros on our backs and I was thankful they weren't mules or horses. They'd have beaten us to death.

Time ceased to mean anything and my nerves began to wear thin. Phil remained the same teak-faced sphinx except for rare smiles for some of the Mayans who were even more tireless and sphinx-like. Hours would pass without them saying a word and not once did any of them utter a complaint or express a desire to be in the sunlight again. We followed Pepé's black paint marks and stumbled onward, trying to be quiet but never quite making it.

Then came the day or night when we were pulled to a halt by the sight of a man sitting bolt upright in a niche about ten feet above our traveling level. That would put him above water level, too. He sat so upright that he was certainly stiff dead and the dark spot between his eyes and red icicle hanging from the end of his nose told part of the story. Phil supplied the rest out of his fertile imagination. "He's a guard. Pepé crept up on him out of the dark and I'll bet he started to light a cigarette." He scampered up the steep face of the slating dripstone, picked up something and came back. He held it up. "End just scorched," he said, grinning.

"But why would Pepé shoot him? Looks like that would have given an alarm."

Phil smote his hands together sharply. The sound fell dead. "It wouldn't have been heard a hundred feet. Caverns like this are famous for such peculiarities. I think we'll rest here and wait a while. Pepé probably is on his way back."

I had begun to think of Phil as something of a seer and especially now—Pepé crept into our rest spot in less than thirty minutes.

He squatted and started speaking in Spanish, making excited gestures with his hands. For fifteen minutes he talked and answered questions, then Phil turned to me. "Well, here we are."

"Are we? Where?"

"Five more miles then you'll see something you've never seen before. A subterranean cavern, a regular deepwater harbor. Not very wide but wide enough to accommodate a small freighter that has been converted into a sort of pinch-hit destroyer. Five-inch thirty-eight caliber guns, I'd say from Pepé's description. And two submarines."

I sat trying to figure this deal out while the chatter between Pepé and Soldarez continued apace.

Finally Phil turned to me. "There's one more thing and in case it strikes you by surprise I don't want a startled yell out of you at an inopportune moment."

"I don't startle like that," I scoffed.

"Well, that's fine. They have Verna."

I uttered a peep like a bedraggled duckling drowning in a cloud-burst and nearly fainted. "They ... they ... they ..."

"They!" He completed for me. "I'm glad your yells of surprise are in a minor key. It improves matters no end."

We got moving then—cautiously, you can bet—and after a hard two hours of travel Phil stopped us. He hissed experimentally and nodded with satisfaction. "Dead spot. Tether the burros here," he told the Mayans, "out of sight here in this corridor. They can bray all they want to there. Unpack the boat, sub gun and ammo drums and for God's sake don't leave the tire pump."

Pepé attended to every detail himself. All this time I stayed as numb a freshly mashed finger, trying to figure the angles. They'd gotten her to get at me but how had she beaten us to the spot? I gave up, shook my head clear and in a fashion forgot about that part of the case. I'd need all my faculties. Besides the sub gun two carbines came from the pack. Phil took one and handed me the other. "Six filled magazines," he said. "You take three and I'll take three."

"Who gets the chopper?"

"I'll let one of the Mayans carry it. I brought it along as added security. Maybe we won't need it."

"With all that ammo and you just brought it along for kicks," I sneered.

I took my medicine and we started forward, single file. I lost track of time until at last in the distance I heard the sounds of activity and smelled coal smoke. The musical clink of a hammer on an anvil, the crash of a length of chain dropped, other discordant noises all blended into something that sounded like any dockside activity.

Motioning to the others to stay twenty paces behind, Phil beckoned to me and together we walked in the direction of the sounds. Putting his mouth to my ear he whispered very softly. "I think all the area around here is dead accoustically, possibly because the rocks are coated with salt, but we can't be sure. Certainly the noises from ahead aren't magnified to any great extent. Now, this may be the only entrance to the dock area from the cavern. If it is there will surely be one guard there, maybe more. Pepe didn't try to find out. As soon as he could see what was going on he stopped, looked, then came on back. Okay, let's go."

We went ahead and I silently gave Pepé a vote of extreme confidence. When we finally came to a place where we could see I was clear about a lot of things. First, I wondered what they did about the tides. Then I saw that we were some twenty feet below the level of a shelf that was wide enough for a B-29, curving around the water to the right; it was lighted as bright as day by hundreds of electric bulbs. To the left I could see nothing because our corridor didn't meet the area head on but at an angle. Furthermore, I could see that the tide would be funneled straight into several consecutive exits wider than the one we occupied. Either they hadn't relieved the guard yet or they were fools because there were no sentries about the mouth of our corridor. Almost before I got the words through my thought channels we heard the scrape of leather against stone. Phil motioned fiercely and backed behind a boulder. I tried to find one, couldn't, and fell flat as far out of the way as possible. Even so, the eggs almost hatched. The guy, a thickset German like a twin of Loder, swung his flash and saw me. He opened his mouth only to close it with a snap as the butt of Phil's carbine smashed the base of his skull like a ripe papaya.

"Unnecessarily hard, I suppose," he said, breath whistling through his nose.

I didn't agree worth a damn but I nodded. "Just the same we don't have time to go around tying people up. They get loose and become an enemy behind your back."

He motioned to me and we stepped out into the main cavern housing a little deep-water bay.

We had to climb a flight of steps to get to the shelf that spread as far on the left as the other one did on the right. Separating the shelves was a stretch of calm black water a good hundred feet wide and, from the sheer sides of the shelves, probably as deep close in as in the middle.

Further down, near a rakish little craft that had the high poop of a small freighter, was a beehive of activity. The destroyer had given some back if not as much as it had absorbed. The bridge and fantail were twisted mangled tangles of cables, smashed lifeboats and superstructure.

Acetelyne torches flared and squirted sparks like Roman candles, electric arcs flickered and flared like summer lightning. Hustling hither and yon, carrying tools, torches and otherwise occupied, were numbers of men.

Phil pointed. "Dead area. We were closer than we thought and there's a hell of a racket going on down there."

"Goody ... I think."

"Quite and all that sort of rot. Thing is, can we make them run for the open sea?"

"Sure. We build a sailboat, put a satchel charge on it, blow gently on it with our whiskey breaths and into the midst of them it'll go unnoticed and blow everything to hell and gone. What's left will be glad to make for the sea."

To my surprise he nodded grimly. "Not a bad idea—on an ebbing tide. We just don't have a satchel charge. Dammit, I didn't know what to expect and I find myself rather overwhelmed by the fact now."

I grunted. "Well, let's kill off a few. They can't hear anything with all that racket."

His hard face grew harder. "That's not a bad idea. I doubt, with you, that anything can be heard over that noise. Now," he mused, squinting his eyes against the glare of the lights, "whom shall it be?"

"That gizmo with the blue jacket looks like a pusher or an officer or something. Pot him and I'll take the guy with the blueprints talking to him."

He looked at his sights. "Is that over a hundred and fifty yards?"

"No. Less, I'd say. Not too much less, though."

"Okay, aim at the part in his hair and you'll hit the back of the neck." He turned to the Mayans and Spanished them back to Pepé.

We rested our rifles on the rough face of the rock where our heads projected over it.

"None of this business of firing together," he said. "You can't be accurate like that. You first and I'll come right behind you."

"Right." I brought the blueprints chap into the peep, crept the bead up until it was lined right at the button on his cap and I squeezed one off carefully. Right in my ear came Phil's shot and two men were motionless on the floor of the cavern. For a moment or two no one noticed it; then a worker paused in full stride, gawked, dropped an armful of tools and bent over.

In ten seconds the place was thick with men.

"Empty your piece," said Phil calmly. "Not too fast and right into the thick of them."

Two bullets a second and none of them could miss but the last three had to be aimed carefully because the men started scattering before we were empty.

"That'll give them something to think about," said Phil, cramming a fresh magazine in his rifle.

"Maybe this will give you something to think about," said a voice immediately behind us.

CHAPTER THIRTEEN

W E SPUN AROUND to see two men, one obviously a
German sailor and the other a thin starved-faced man
who might have been anything. Lugers were trained at our mid-
dles and there was nothing to do but drop our rifles as the thin
man had ordered.

They marched us up to the top of the rim and gestured
toward the ships where heads were beginning to show cautiously
around corners.

"Like ducks in a rain barrel," I said glumly.

"Worse," said Phil with a trace of bitterness. "No duck will
put himself in a rain barrel. We did. Too interested in our own
private executions."

"There will be other executions," put in the little man behind
us. "After a fair trial, naturally."

"Naturally," I said with false heartiness.

"Of course. There will be confessions and other sport."

I went a little cold at that but I was in for a fair store of sur-
prises. The first was the sight of Dr. Moffett treating the wounded,
but I noted with satisfaction that there were more dead than
wounded and plenty of both. What surprised me was that I had
the doctor picked as the big man and there he was scrabbling
around in the blood and filth like a common sawbones.

Another shock was the sight of Verna standing at the rail of
the little converted freighter and looking at the carnage. I had
expected to see her a prisoner, too. She hadn't seen us as yet, and
I wasn't too anxious for her to go through a Dayne sequence

and make me sicker than I already was. One thing was certain, I was already sick to a degree that made my head wonder where the hell the rest of me was. Between that and the situation we were in I wasn't much good to anyone. I was all scrambled in the head without the ability to do any thinking; otherwise I'd never have pulled the fool stunt I did. I suppose the misery and the natural fear that the end of the line was swiftly approaching just goaded me past the limits of my tolerance. I whirled like a cat and pounced on the little guy, snatched the Luger out of his hand and sank it out of sight in his head. Then something, from the feel of it, went out of sight in mine.

I came to sprawled on my face against smooth cool drip-stone. I was conscious of one simple thing—if something didn't ease my head death would cease all pain and anguish. It seemed to pulsate and breathe; each beat of my heart was a sledge hammer coated with rubber that didn't smash with sharp hard pain but shook me all the way to the toenails with raging flood tides of agony.

I sat up and fell over before I could catch myself. My balance was gone because the floor tilted and I scraped my nails on the floor until my fingers were raw and bleeding. Phil, apparently sensing what was wrong, sat on my legs and that was all that kept me from falling off into some awful black void. Thankfully, I passed out again and when I came to some of the pain was gone but I was still in bad shape. I vomited luxuriously and immediately felt better but I sure stank up our prison. I managed to remain sitting for a while and got my eyes into focus to find our room a small thing about forty feet in diameter with one opening. One guard sat smack in it and conversed with another immediately on the outside.

"Feeling better?" asked Phil.

"I feel like hell," I muttered, even my jaws aching when I talked. "This is the last, I do mean the last time I'll ever trust a woman. It is the last time I'll ever pull a dippy stunt like I did chopping that little runt."

"That may well be," said Phil, prophetically. "I understand we're to be tried today—or tonight, whichever is now. Some madman must be leading this outfit to even bother with a trail, especially when the verdict has already been handed down."

"What has happened since I took my snooze?"

"Nothing. The Kraut wanted me to start something too, so he could stitch me up with that Luger."

"Smart boy. Jesus, how dumb can a man get?"

"As to that, I couldn't say. Why the German didn't shoot you instead of banging you on the dome, I don't know. I expected to see him fill you full of bullets."

"I'm glad I didn't stay conscious long enough to do any speculating on it. How long have we been here?"

"Twenty hours, by my time. The guard will no doubt relay the news of your recovery, which is what they've been waiting for, to the proper authorities. And then comes the trial."

"By the way, have you located the cache of gold and diamonds?"

Phil let loose a short ugly laugh. "Hardly. I've been somewhat restricted in my activities."

About thirty minutes later the guard in the entrance stood and beckoned to us. "Out."

He was respectful. He walked twenty feet behind us with his rifle held at the ready and marched up opposite the sub that lay tied up opposite the freighter—and I saw that in some manner we had crossed the water obstacle and were on the opposite side from where we had been surprised.

A bunch of hard-faced men stood about with their eyes filled with verdict and my mental projector began to flash the good things of life through my mind like mad. What is death, I asked myself? A flash of pain, a struggle for breath or a numbness that anesthetizes the normal reaction to the point where you can spend your last few seconds being philosophical? I felt outraged at people who tried to make death something beautiful and enticing. To a hopeless sufferer maybe it would be beautiful like a cheap new watch in a mud hole; relative. To me, right then, the most beautiful thing in the world was a shapeless thing called life. Something you couldn't picture except by analogy, arraying all the delightful sensuous experiences in order and enjoying them in prospect. It was beginning to seem that the only thing left to us was retrospect and little time for that. The guard stood us up about twenty feet from a canvas folding chair and backed out of the way, still letting the muzzle of his rifle stare at us.

Some twenty men stood on either side of the chair, apparently awaiting the chief justice. That would be something, just to see who he was.

He came finally and sat in the chair, a very different picture from what he was when we had first seen him. Phil muttered something under his breath and I felt like an utter fool looking at a discovery I'd been using as a toothpick. Jonathan sat in the chair and looked at us, his eyes brand new in his face because now they were the cold deadly eyes of a dangerous, immensely calculating man. Maybe a little touched in the onion. He sure looked it.

"Greetings," he said through stiff lips. A smile bent the flesh around his mouth like a bulldozer bending a tin shack. "I'm really very glad to see you, gentlemen. You especially, Mister Markham. I dislike being patronized. I further dislike being treated like a small child."

What did I have to lose? "You were acting like one," I pointed out in a voice stronger in sound than the courage backing it up.

The smile again. I listened for the sound of it, like lava hissing into the sea, but no sound effects. "Regrettably a part of the act. And, of course, you are correct. I was rather good, don't you think?"

"Very," I said. "I take it we're up for trial?"

"Oh, no. To receive sentence." He turned to the men and asked, "Gentlemen of the jury, what say you?"

"Death." It was repeated in three or four tongues, all understandable.

"*Morte.*"

"*Muerte.*"

"*Tod.*"

He turned back to us. "The verdict is unanimous. Unfortunately you killed and wounded quite a number of men, some almost irreplaceable. You aren't by any chance a shipfitter are you, Mr. Markham?"

"Nope. I'm a fit tester."

"I beg your pardon?"

"I test the fit of garments, preferably those of women. I may say that Verna's fit was flawless."

His face flushed red. "Mr. Markham, we don't have to shoot you in a vital spot, you know. We could shoot you in the guts. I did my commanding officer that favor after I decided to desert from the Army and make my own way in the world. He was seriously inconvenienced for several days."

"I take it all back," I said as sarcastically as I could.

He ignored me. "You, Captain Soldarez, the eminent white card man, our twentieth century Robin Hood, are you possessed of any particular talent which might cause us temporarily to spare you?"

A sardonic smile twisted the piratical face. "I doubt it. I am particularly adept at killing chickens. I can wring the neck of a cockerel with one twist. I doubt that you'd benefit from such a talent."

Red dyed the face of the hard youngster again. "I admire such talents greatly but admiration must give way to expediency this once. Just the same I wonder if you are as good as you think you are?"

"Probably twice as good as that," said Phil with a diabolical grin.

Jonathan turned to a man. "Go fetch Ernst. We will have some amusement before we witness the execution."

There were grins among the spectators as the man hurried away to fetch Ernst.

Phil spoke again. "Since we are to be liquidated I wonder if you would grant us the favor of enlightening our brains which will soon grow dark?"

"Gladly. Just what would you like to know?"

"Give me a brief history of your activities since shooting Colonel Larkspur at Salerno."

There was a quick gasp all around and Jonathan went white, but only for a moment. When he remembered that this piece of information was likely to die in a moment he recovered. "What an upsetting man you are, Captain. How nice it is to have you standing where you are." He stood up and began to pace up and down nervously. "It all began when I was a First Lieutenant in Salerno. Colonel Larkspur and I had graduated from O.C.S. in the same class. I was under him from then on. He was a man of no particular talents, no special intelligence but up he went in leaps and bounds." He glanced at me. "He, too, was given to patronization and he made a show of trying to get me moved along in rank, but I knew what went on in his head. He knew where his greatest danger lay. He knew that were it not for his amazing proclivity for kowtowing it would be I who was Colonel and not himself."

He certainly had it turned exactly backward. At that moment I knew him for what he was. I also saw the last glimmer of hope wink out like a match at midnight a mile away.

"So on one particularly bad day when I had taken all I could I shot him in the belly and walked off." He chuckled grimly. "They've often wondered where I was."

"The official report mentioned that Larkspur had been shot in the back." said Phil gently.

Jonathan's eyes grew mad and he made a cat-like motion toward us but stopped. "A collection of damnable lies. I pulled my pistol and shot him at close range."

"The report stated that he had been shot in the back with a .30 caliber carbine bullet."

Jonathan's face went white. "I can see that you and your friend wish to provide us with more entertainment than we had anticipated."

"Probably," mused Phil, looking over his head. "A man who'd shoot another in the back from a safe range wouldn't stop at torturing a helpless prisoner."

I thought Jonathan would throw a fit at that but he interrupted it midway and smiled one of his insane travesties. "Ah, but the way you hurl darts. To continue, I became the head of the black market in Italy with a price on my head from two governments. Then through my own intelligence pipe lines I heard of Captain Walther Von Brock who had escaped in one of the newer types of submarines. We met and came to an agreement. He was the victim of one of your first shots. By an extremely clever coup we lifted a sub from under the very noses of the United States Navy. We even thought of capturing the American destroyer we damaged but our meager facilities here wouldn't have been equal to repairing it. We hope to do better when we move our base. Now, Captain Soldarez, maybe you would like to tell me what you know."

"We know that you intend to dump a terrific lump of gold on the market and try to uproot world economy. Diamonds also."

Jonathan smiled. "You know very little, actually. The diamonds we will use merely as a nuisance to fat comfortable Nederlanders and Belgians, not to mention a few Americans and Britishers. The gold, however, is going to Red China, a condition which you no doubt see will avail us better than the questionable wisdom of trying to break a world market with our little cache. We have a great deal of it, true, but I'm afraid it would be no more than a slight shock, a nuisance, like the diamonds. Financing a country which has limitless manpower and a ruthlessness quite as limitless will be more productive. Think of the business we can do. Don't you agree?"

"Perforce I must," said Phil daintily. "Nevertheless, bucking world governments is a risky business and someone might rob you."

"The danger is certainly real," said Jonathan, "but I'm not afraid for the gold. It is quite safe."

"Where?" I asked.

"I'm afraid I cannot tell you that, Mr. Markham. I can tell you that you caused us to move it from Sierra Negro."

"Tell me one thing," I begged, "How did you pull such a snow job on your parents and Verna's?"

He laughed lightly, happily. "The war, you know. I disappeared. My brother, not a twin either. I was a year older but he looked enough like me for a twin. Such differences as there were the years and rigors of war could explain."

"What happened to your brother?"

"We had a reunion of sorts. There was wassail and debauchery to be enjoyed and unluckily he had a very bad accident. Fatal, in fact, and I saw a chance to take his papers and become him. So I did. He had always been rather an ass. Holding up that part of the act was my most difficult obstacle. But I managed it."

"Beautifully," I said.

"Thank you, Mr. Markham. You will live five minutes longer for that sneer. Our problem will be to keep you alive long enough to live out your sentence—if you get what I mean."

"I'm pretty sharp today." At that point a hulking German walked around the spectators and saluted Jonathan.

"Ah, the good Ernst. Ernst, the tall and improbably smooth gentleman over there has stated that he is about twice as good as I think he is. I thought possible you might show him to be in error."

The thick man said something in a guttural undertone and nodded. Then he stripped off his shoes and shirt. Phil went him one better. He stripped down until he wore nothing but a pair of tight cotton jockey shorts. I thought I might discover some flaw in his physique when he stripped but I didn't, from the delicate arches of his feet to the gentle classicism of his neck he was a dream in smooth tan sculpture. Nowhere did he lump or bulge except when a flash of effort flicked through his muscles; then his skin was silk over steel cables. He flexed his arms and made a single limbering circle of them, throwing symmetrical snakes of muscle into momentary definition. He was ready then.

Ernst was a strong man. No one could deny that. His arms were heavy with tremendous biceps and his stomach was roped with heavy layers of rock-hard flesh and muscle. His back was a thick corded mass that moved with his actions like live serpents.

They moved together and Phil circled, balancing on the balls of his feet like a dancer. Here was brute strength facing exquisite conditioning and split-second coordination. But the Kraut still looked mighty formidable to me. He looked as dentless as the sides of a battle ship.

"I might mention, Captain," said Jonathan, smiling, "that Ernst is one of the strongest men in the world. He can break a man's back with ease. If he ever gets his hands on you... Save some of him, Ernst. We'll need him for other uses when you're through.

"I safe som off him," said Ernst, grinning.

"I saw him break a man's neck once, Captain." His jaw dropped and for good reason.

Like a tiger Soldarez sprang in and ripped a rocketing left followed by a neck-jolting right to Ernst's huge chin. The blows sounded like socking a block of ice with the back of an axe and Ernst did what many a good man would have done. He sat down with shocking force on his fanny, looking pretty stupid. Phil stood a few feet away, his hands on his slim hips, balanced, ready and graceful with a grin of Satan on his mocking face.

"I beg your pardon," he said to Jonathan. "I didn't get that last feat of strength that Ernst performed."

Jonathan, red and choking, clenched his fists at his sides. "Get up and murder that grinning ape, Ernst, else I have something special for you."

Ernst seemed to like it where he was, as though it was cool down there on a hot day. He shook his head carefully and started slowly to his feet. When almost erect he lunged forward and grabbed Phil in a bear hug and began to strain him closer. Phil's back didn't seem any easier to break down than an I-beam; then I saw why. He had placed both fists against Ernst's abdomen with his elbows resting against his own and Ernst's might was thrown right back into his own stomach. Ernst's face grew purple from the effort and Phil became a rigid bronze statue, his magnificent musculature etched against his skin like the lines of a woodcut. I felt a laugh of relief shake me way down.

Ernst was strong but so was Phil and my boy was six times as agile. A hard knee came up like an exploding piston and though Ernst managed to catch it on a hip, a lump the size of a baseball sprang into being and a strained groan came from the big man's throat.

Phil's right hand leaped out of its hiding place and smashed Ernst beneath the left ear with a chop that sent him reeling away, his eyes wandering about without direction. He missed a badly placed step and crashed to the rock floor. He didn't get up right away.

Phil stood easily to one side, his grin unchanged, his arms crossed over his chest. "Was Ernst doing a job of work when you interrupted him?" he asked Jonathan.

Jonathan nodded dazedly, watching the man's efforts to reach his feet.

"In that case maybe we'd better end this charming dance, else he might not be able to finish it."

So he ended it. When Ernst came to his feet Phil swarmed him with short killing blows, blows that jarred him all the way to his toenails. Then he was backed to the wall where Phil measured him with repeated brutal smashes. But the man's vitality was such that although out he was still on his feet. Finally Phil stepped back a pace, flexed his shoulders and sent in a whistling right uppercut that almost tore Ernst's head from his shoulders. He fell forward and almost like a dying reflex a sluggish left went out and struck Phil a very weak blow in the stomach.

The effect was astonishing. Phil reeled back as though he had been kicked by a mule and before anyone knew what was happening he turned right on the edge of the rock rim and dived into the black water.

CHAPTER FOURTEEN

FOR A MOMENT everyone remained frozen; then Jonathan leaped forward and began to scream orders at the top of his voice. Soon his lips were flecked with a mad froth and his eyes were burning wells of insane light. And right in the middle of it he folded up like a sack of mud and stretched out on the stone floor of the cavern. All hands stopped, frozen in their tracks, and before they could move three of them lay kicking on the floor, the only sound having been that of the wicked *snaaak* of high-powered bullets. When they did move they moved fast and walked right into a gallon or so of slugs vomited from a Schmeisser sub-pistol. Down they went like straw before a mower. Stone splinters stung me where I stood but miraculously none of the slugs got me.

My guard threw his rifle as far as he could and started screaming *"Kamerad! Kamerad!"*

I picked it up and walked over to the guy who had slugged me and tried to tear his face off with a vertical butt stroke that I crammed every ounce of my heft into.

"I seem to have heard those words of surrender before some place," said a gaunt leathery demon as he came out from his grotto where he had been out of sight. The snout of the Schmeisser still trailed a tendril of smoke. He was starved-looking, his clothes were in tatters and he was so covered with grime and chlorophyl from crushed leaves that he looked positively bilious.

"Jesus Christ," I breathed. "Norcross."

"Right, my frozen-footed friend. Why didn't you follow Soldarez into the drink?"

"Because I'm so muddled I don't know my name." A thought struck me and I whirled to see Pepé and the Mayans coming at a dead run across the opposite rim of rock. A head showed above the tower of the sub and Pepé drilled it without even breaking his stride. As it disappeared I heard the thump and saw the short deadly chopper he had carried as it skated across the tiny deck and fell into the water.

Then Verna, clad in nothing much, dived from the bridge of the little freighter and swam toward us. I helped her out and crushed her trembling body against me and forgot the hell about wars of all sorts. I even forgot that for a while I had suspected her of being another, but shrewder Dayne.

Two hours later things were fairly shipshape. Phil had crawled up on the whaleback of the sub as soon as he saw things were inclining our way. The corpses had been sewn in canvas and their effects packaged. They were to be left until a destroyer could reach the spot. Norcross, who discovered among his talents the ability to handle the converted freighter's radio, had already made contact and even now a lean greyhound of the seas was tearing toward Cabo Blanco under forced draught. We had herded the prisoners into the dark forward hold of the freighter along with those of the wounded who could make it. Those too badly wounded stayed topside on cots with our Mayans guarding them. They had the certain knowledge that they would be shot in their tracks if they tried anything because one had made a break and was shot through the head as he went over the side. If there were any other malingerers they didn't make it known.

Norcross came back from inspecting the ventilation in the hold and grinned at us. "Well, you fellows did it."

"Who're you trying to kid?" I asked with a scowl.

"Double that," said Phil who was taking time out to dress. "I was safe after a fashion in the water but the best I could have done was escape. How did you find the entrance?"

Norcross slumped wearily against a winch cover. "I did it the hard way. I wondered a few times if I'd make it. Yucatan's jungle doesn't reach the sky but it plays hell on the ground."

"How long will it take the destroyer to get here?" asked Phil.

"Captain Hammond of the *O'Rourke,* the can I talked to, says he's something like two hundred miles south by southeast and logging thirty knots."

"I had thought," said Phil, "that since we had Miss Martell we should start back through the cave. But if the destroyer is that close I think we should bum a ride to Progresso."

All was well. Navies went back to their respective bases and shipping company officials went back to pinching secretaries at propitious moments and ulcers healed miraculously. But—this was a but big enough to launch an international treasure hunt the like of which ain't been seen yet—we hadn't located the hoard of bullion. The men stoutly swore that the gold had been carried into the cave by outside workmen who had been imported to do the job. It was wrapped to prevent any knowledge of the contents and Jonathan and von Brock were the only ones accompanying them. Narco-synthesis failed to aid in the questioning. We dragged the cave harbor but come up with nothing but boulders.

We went back to Chichen and stashed ourselves away in the Mayaland Lodge where we sat around sipping *Carta Clara* and/or drinks of other sorts, letting our wonderful minds plough up the turf of speculation; but it was either pretty barren soil or our minds weren't up to my advertisement.

Señors Barbachano, Junior and Senior wandered in and out of the Lodge. They were dividing their time between Merida, Uxmal, where another lodge was in the process of erection, and Chichen; they appeared to have lost their former concern about business.

Over drinks before dinner one night Fernando, looking like a rather jaunty interne in his white *guayabera* and pale blue slacks had this to say about the state of their good spirits.

"It's understandable, Ches. One look at our reservation list would convince you. The world knows about us now and I'm hoping that among the visitors will be a man who won't mind spending a million or so in further exploration and restoration. The surface has barely been scratched."

At dinner, Soldarez was brilliant, Fernando, Junior was witty and charming, Norcross was taciturn as usual, Verna was positively scintillant in a creation of powder blue that very effectively kept my mind from such crass matters as hoards of bullion. And things of that sort. Then, right out of the blue I blurted, "Tracks."

Phil, who can pitch his eyebrows like an expert pitching horseshoes, pitched one and made me blush, I felt so foolish.

Norcross's hard mouth twitched in a smile. "Did you say tracks?"

I'd loved to have chucked the whole thing but I was committed so I resolved to make it as good as I could.

"Tracks," I repeated. "Remember, Phil? The only place where they showed was in the first cavern around the foot of the *Castillo* and out toward the *cenote*."

"That's right," he agreed. "The rest of the cave is too hard for tracks. I imagine that dust washed down there before the pyramid was sealed off."

"Well, it just popped into my mind. There were a regular parade of tracks around the *cenote* and very few where we went in. How come?"

Phil went rigid. Norcross already was, his face as expressionless as a mask. Verna didn't get it and didn't care too much one way or the other. Fernando drew in his breath with a sibilant hiss.

For a few seconds there was dead silence and then everyone started talking at once. Finally when quiet was restored Norcross

said. "Phil, this is your part of the world. Can you make arrange-
ments to have the *cenote* dredged?"

"I can and will. Tomorrow we should start. However, I suggest that a diver be sent down to see what's there first. There's no
need to dredge the place unless the stuff is there."

Fernando laughed. "I don't agree with you but I see your
point. We'd love to have the *cenote* explored because I, for one,
do not believe that Edward Thompson got any more than a token
of what is really there."

That night plans were made and the phone wires stayed hot
half the night. Those who say that Mexico's telephones are slower
than pony express ought to see a man like Phil work out on them.

The next day about noon a diver from Progresso with full
rig was lowered into the jade depths of the *cenote* and didn't stay
down ten minutes. He landed right on top of it and judging from
his excitement when he came up the bottom must have been
paved with it. The diamonds were in sealed tarred tins and the
ingots of gold were wrapped carefully with burlap and tied with
binder twine. I'd tell you how much we recovered except that it's
a state secret, plus the fact that when you see a regular pyramid
of the stuff all in one place you lose your perspective. I'm good at
figures but not that kind.

The American Consul, anxious to be the first to congratulate us on our coup, pitched a whingding for the lot of us. Phil
and Norcross, however, had evaporated, which left me to do the
honors and my attention was so divided that I didn't do very well
by them. After the affair, during which Verna and I managed to
get faintly plastered, we started for Tulipanes; but we never got
there. With her soft lips driving me wild and her fabulous body
a bouquet of madness neither she nor I could stand the idea of
putting off our visit to the little *parque*. It was the same and again
the moon had come into being and flooded the place with pure
white light.

She stood straight, her arms about my waist, her body hugging mine so close that I could feel her heart beat. "Ches, did you doubt me very long?"

"Not very, but it was a hard doubt. Damn, I've never even asked how he got you."

"By the simple ruse of sending me a note to come to the Ball Court and signing your name to it. I'd never seen your writing and he was smart enough to figure that out. Of course, that cornfield that you and Phil found, down that road where you and Felipe were taken that night, was being used for a helicopter landing. That's how I got to the place before you did. They knew I couldn't escape and no one was afraid of me so I was left alone."

"Did he try anything?"

Her eyes were somber and serious. "That's why he kidnaped me."

I felt a hell boiling inside me. "Did he succeed?"

"Yes."

My fingers were numb from the fury that was trying to choke me. "Didn't you fight him?"

"What good would it have done there, Ches? All I'd have gotten was a bad beating and he'd have won anyway. I'm not spoiled or ruined or anything."

I nodded dumbly. "Of course not, kid. The thought makes me want to kill, that's all. I'll never mention it again." And I didn't.

Again in the moonlight her gorgeous body gradually lost its obscuring clothing and finally she stood there slim and beautiful beyond my wildest dreams, an earthly goddess of the purest reality as fragrant as frangipani and as soft as its petals. She was an offering to the rites of man's closest approach to divinity, the nearest he can reach to heaven in this sphere. She was a smooth writhing snake whose gushing breath was a measure of the depth of her feeling, whose exorbitant performance was a guide to the heights she could reach.

"Ches ..." For a moment she held me so tightly that I couldn't breathe. "Ches ... darling ... like snow in a landslide ..." She gave a single titanic heave and screamed into the flesh of my neck, locked me in a convulsive grip and then—as consummation reached her—she fainted.

The Constellation disgorged passengers from South America and Guatemala while we stood on the second story terrace in the busy airport terminal and watched. Lonzo—irked, I think, because the departure yanked him out of the arms of a lusty maiden in Progresso—stood apart and sulked.

"We've got to come back, Ches," Verna said as we watched the people stream into the terminal.

"Often," I said. "Think of never seeing people like Felipe, José, the Barbachanos again. I guess it is inevitable that we barge into Phil some place."

"The most inevitable thing you ever heard of," came a voice from behind us, laced with a hint of piratical laughter.

We spun around and it was the great man himself, debonair, as slick as a movie poster in a dazzling uniform and boots that shone like polished metal. He clicked his heels and bowed. "I hope such open admiration is deserved."

"There can be little doubt of that," said Verna laughing. "Did a fly ever try to land on you?"

"The word got around that it was a hazardous project and they stopped trying."

"Going back to the States?" I asked.

"Yes. The eighth child of my seventh uncle, a darling female of eighteen, has issued a formal ultimatum that I be present at some adolescent party she is giving and since duties at home do not press I am winging my way there. I have always admired the women of New Orleans."

"New Orleans ... Soldarez ... Surely not Lolita Soldarez?" Verna was excited.

"Almost. Lolita is practically ancient. She is all of twenty. Evangelina is younger but equally potent. You know them, I take it."

"I should say so. They live right across Nashville Avenue in front of our house."

"Ah, so? Then I'd say our delightful association is not at an immediate end. Neither of you are curious, I suppose, about the end of this affair?"

He had to practically fight us off so he started the windup. "First, Dr. Moffett was indeed a member of the gang. Also, he had discovered things about the Mayans no one else ever knew. Bishop Landa burned their books but in those rooms in the caves are more books than Landa ever saw. Moffett was also an expert on hieroglyphics and rooted out the secret of the Ball Courts. He used the man whose body we found as an experiment to see if the story was true since they intended to liquidate him anyway. I'd say it was pretty well true."

"Almost," I conceded.

"The Barbachanos are undertaking a total exploration of the cave and have found plenty, believe me. They intend to make a museum in the cave proper. I understand Hollywood is interested not only because the story reads like something from Sax Rhomer but because of the sound effects in the cave. They're looking for a likely male lead," he added roguishly.

"In that case they need look no further," I said.

He was faintly astonished. "You mean you'd take it?"

"No, but you'd make Errol Flynn look like Donald Meek. You'd be perfect for the part."

For the first time in my acquaintance with him, Phil blushed like a school girl and we both enjoyed a good laugh at his expense. I wiped my eyes. "One more thing. How did you know that Jonathan was Jonathan Fuller of Salerno infamy?"

"Norcross told me about him the time I flew him to Yugoslavia. He had tried to find him but failed. He had a photo of him and all the time at the hotel I hadn't paid the boy a great deal of attention. Only when he mentioned what he had done to his C.O. in Salerno did the recognition occur."

I sighed. "Well, it was an extremely nasty business and I'm glad I'm on my way back."

The loudspeaker came alive and passengers began to saunter out toward the plane so we joined them.

The henequen farms slid beneath us, the matted green of the jungle and finally the white sliver of beach seemed to wave to us as we roared out into the vast indigo waste that was the Gulf of Mexico.

We were going home; life was pretty great.

THE END